CRACKS

CRACKS

->-><-<-

Sheila Kohler

Z

ZOLAND BOOKS
Cambridge, Massachusetts

First edition published in 1999 by
Zoland Books, Inc.
384 Huron Avenue
Cambridge, Massachusetts 02138

Copyright © 1999 by Sheila Kohler

Parts of this novel were previously published in a
different version in *The Paris Review, Bomb,* and *The KGB Bar Reader.*

FIRST PAPERBACK EDITION

Book design by Boskydell Studio
Printed in the United States of America

05 04 03 02 01 00   8 7 6 5 4 3 2 1

This book is printed on acid-free paper, and its binding materials
have been chosen for strength and durability.

Library of Congress Cataloging-in-Publication Data
Kohler, Sheila
Cracks : a novel / Sheila Kohler. — 1st ed.
p.   cm.
ISBN 1-58195-008-x (cloth)
ISBN 1-58195-026-8 (paper)
I. Title.
PR9369.3.K65C7   1999
823 — dc21   99-27263
CIP

This book is for my beloved husband Bill,
without whose fortitude, intelligence and hard work
none of this would have been possible.

I have been helped enormously over the years in the revising of my work by a number of people whom I have never thanked properly:

Jeanette Perrette, who sat and listened at length after lunch while I haltingly translated my words into French.

Karen Satran, who provided friendship, food, advice — and even a husband.

Stephen McCauley, who would lean forward along the table and say, "Well I liked the passage about. . . ." and for his letters and consistent kindness.

Amy Hempel, who kept me writing with her support and generosity and wisdom.

Therese Svoboda, Victoria Redel, Diane Williams, Lily Tuck, Suzanne McNear, Rebecca Kavaler, Blair Birmelin, Patty Dann, Diane DeSanders, Sondra Olsen, Gay Walley.

Others whose support has been crucial: William Abrahams, Dawn Raffel, Elizabeth Gaffney, Mark Mirsky, and Patrick McGrath.

My agent Robin Straus.

And my darling girls: Sasha, Cybele, and Brett, who are my best readers.

Bring me my Bow of burning gold:
Bring me my Arrows of desire:
Bring me my Spear: O Clouds unfold!
Bring me my Chariot of fire.

— William Blake, *Milton*

The Thirteen Girls
on the Swimming Team

FUZZIE BURLS

FIAMMA CORONNA

JULIE DENCH

MEG DONOVAN

SHEILA KOHLER

ANN LINDT, VICE CAPTAIN

DI RADFIELD, CAPTAIN

PAMELA RICHTER

MARY SKEEN

SANDRA SWANN

BOBBY JEAN TREVELYAN

BOBBY JOE TREVELYAN

LIZZIE TURNER

The Staff

MISS SUNNY NIEVEN, M.A. OXFORD,
HEADMISTRESS

MISS G, SWIMMING
MISS LACEY, ENGLISH
MRS. WILLIS, SCIENCE
MRS. KEILLY, GEOGRAPHY
JOHN MAZABOKO, NIGHT WATCHMAN
MRS. LOONEY, MATRON

PART ONE

REUNION

✦✦✦

There was Di Radfield, our captain,
So rich and bold and fair.
She wore her blouse wide open
And a pin in her hay-colored hair.

Ann Lindt was the one with the brain.
She was sallow-skinned and lean.
Of Fiamma's friends she was the main,
The vice captain of our swimming team.

Fuzzie differed from the norm
With her curly hair and strange mind.
She sang madrigals at night in the dorm.
She was odd, perhaps, but kind.

Meg Donovan had a pretty face.
An R.C., like all five Donovan girls,
She was full of sultry grace
With her heavy, red lips and her soft, dark curls.

Sheila Kohler, too, was there.
She wrote it down for us.
She watched with her blue-gray stare.
She was interested in lust.

But the one Miss G loved best
Was the one who came from afar.
It was the thirteenth girl who was put to the test:
Fiamma, the princess, our languid swimming star.

The graves of Sir George Harrow and his faithful bullterrier, Jock

THE WHITE SKY meets the flatness of the plain, pressing down heavily all around. In front of the school nothing moves except the shimmer of heat. It is all distance: flat land, sky, and the slight trace of the river that runs slow and dun beside the graves toward the low, blue hills.

Looking out, so many years later, from the red-roofed buildings of our Dutch-gabled school across terraced lawns and veld toward the river and the wattle trees, we can no longer see the graves, but we can still hear the hum of the mosquitoes that swarm along the banks of the stagnant water. We can still smell the thick smoke of Miss G's cigarette. In our minds' eyes we see Fiamma lying on the gray marble grave beneath the frangipani trees. Her slender hands are crossed on her chest, and the white irises that grow wild along the banks of the river cover her body like candles. A faint breeze stirs the hem of her earth-colored tunic. She seems asleep.

We stand on the veranda, clutching the parapet as if it is the railing of a tossing ship, and gaze at the faint trace of the river, beside which lie the graves of Sir George Harrow and his faithful bullterrier, Jock.

Our school, which was renowned for neither academic excellence nor illustrious alumnae, had once belonged to Sir George, a high commissioner and hero of the Boer War. He distinguished himself at Ladysmith and Kimberley. Even his bullterrier, Jock, was famous for bravery and fidelity. According to legend, he ran a great distance and traversed many dangers in the war-torn veld to summon help for his wounded master. The little lozenge of his grave lies beside Sir George's.

The area around the graves was always out-of-bounds, but we ran there to escape the other girls and pick the purple and white irises, which grew wild by the river. There was a picnic hut with a red, beaten-clay floor and two latrines, which gave off an unholy odor. Vagrants sometimes sheltered there, and we would find their striped blankets and tin mugs under the benches. We would lie in the shade of the frangipanis on Sir George's cool, gray marble grave and cover our bodies with the wild irises and fold our hands on our chests and play dead. We managed to move the heavy marble slab aside enough to gaze down through the crack at the illustrious bones that lay there, white as shells.

The girl in the black shantung

WE WERE SEVENTEEN or eighteen years old, the last time we saw one another. Our world has changed completely: the dormitory called Kitchener is now called Mandela. We have become awkward with one another. We offer up our cheeks to be kissed and then step back, fast. After the first words we stand stiffly in silence with lowered gaze and averted eyes and folded hands. Our breathing alters. Each of us fears the other will notice the changes in us after all these years.

We are careful what we say. Our voices sound odd. The words sound cracked. We have difficulty hearing. We whisper as though someone might overhear. There are silences, clearings of the throat. There is shrill laughter, there are shrill exclamations of delight, professions of surprise. "Not a line, not a wrinkle, my dear, well, only smile marks around the eyes." We do not say that some of the former beauties look old and plain, that some of the once-plain now look youthful and handsome. Nor do we mention that Fiamma is not among us. The subject remains unmentionable among all the bearers of the secret.

Most of the thirteen members of the swimming team are here: Meg Donovan, Ann Lindt, Sheila Kohler. Only Julie Dench and Sandra Swann said they were unable to attend. Even Fuzzie Burls has somehow managed to put in an appearance. She has painted her short, square nails black for the occasion. We have all made some effort at camouflage: we have dressed up, we have masked our faces with heavy makeup, we have donned jewelry. Fingers twist pearls into knots, clutch gold chains, turn watch-bracelets around wrists. Eyes are bloodshot and puffy from the long voyage out.

An impeccably dressed woman in black with a diamond pin in her lapel arrives late, striding firmly across the veranda, her face in the shadows. We do not recognize her at first. Her whole body looks bloated, as if she had soaked up water from all that swimming; even her pebble blue eyes seem watery in her wide face. She is wearing black kid gloves and a double-breasted shantung suit, which makes her sweat.

We are all sweating. We mop the beads from our foreheads. There are rings beneath the arms of our silk blouses, crepe de chine dresses, cotton shirts. One of us pours water from the ice-water jug with the lemon slices.

It has rained the night before, and the brown lawns glisten. A dove coos in a blue gum tree. The late afternoon is still hot, but there is a shift in the weather. Rain threatens again. An eddy of warm air rises with a murmur through the palms, bringing with it the bitter smell of wet zinnias and a distant wail, as of a dreamer's voice, clear and shrill. We fall silent, expectant.

How happy we are to be here. We are all going to have such a *wonderful* time. It is so *nice* that so many have turned up. It is so amazing that some of us have come from so far — Sheila Kohler, all the way from America. How *lucky* for us that the letter from Miss Nieven, our headmistress, was so persuasive. Poor old Miss Nieven: she must be on her last legs by now. Couldn't let the Old Bag die without seeing her one more time. Ann Lindt points out that Miss Nieven had good reason to be persuasive: her tenuous place here, her cottage in the grounds are probably at stake. She and her old school need the money some of us have.

One of us tells the old joke about the parrot and the mustard sandwiches in the brown paper bag, but no one laughs. We leave our sentences unfinished. We ask, "Do you remember how we used to . . ." and then gaze into the distance.

We listen to the grandfather clock in the hall chime the hour. We look at the brass bowl of proteas that collect dust and the narrow staircase that leads from the hall beyond the veranda into the shadows.

In our minds' eyes we see Miss G, our swimming teacher, slender and strong, standing by the staircase in her belted khaki overalls and her shiny brown boots. The balusters cast shadows on her, and her clothes seem striped black-and-white. She has mud on her cheek and boots. She moves her munificent mouth to blow her yellow whistle. She calls us to attention: *Line up, girls, line up.*

After such a long absence the spaces between things have altered, some moving closer together and others farther away. The branches of the jacaranda trees stretch higher toward the sky; the palm fronds are thicker and darker; the once-clipped hibiscus bushes have grown into monstrous, dripping trees. The concrete slabs sag sadly beside the pool. Blood red poppies grow even more wildly among the blue hydrangeas near the round, thatched-roofed changing huts. Low blocks of flats have obliterated much of the veld. The dust roads now are tarred. The free-ranging, flat acres of farmland have been cut up and spotted with small houses. The veld has been fenced, and the long grass, uprooted and planted over.

The rooms do not seem as big as when we first entered here. We are to sleep in the dormitory now called Mandela. We raise our eyebrows and goggle at one another. We remember the hard, narrow beds, the lack of privacy, and the tall Zulu night watchman, John Mazaboko, with his torch that punched holes in the hydrangeas outside the window.

The art room has been torn down and replaced. A water fountain has been installed in the shade by the steps, and a new bench, under the loquat tree. The paneled rooms are still shuttered against the bright light and the heat. The faded reprints of Degas's ballet dancers still line the dusty gray corridors. From the hall rises the polished banister from which Bobby Joe, one of the Trevelyan twins, who was to become an Anglican nun, fell while playing horsie when she was five years old. In the library looms Sir George's portrait. He wears a monocle and looks old and dried out. Beside him hangs the dark painting of his dog, broad-backed, stiff-legged, and panting.

The small black holes where several of us poked the light, oak paneling with iron tongs remain in the common room. "Vandals," Miss Nieven called the perpetrators, whistling every time she pronounced an *s*: they pillaged, raped, and burned.

We walk down the wisteria-covered pergola that borders the edge of the perfects' lawn, past what was Miss Nieven's study. Fuzzie walks a little behind the rest of us with her odd, catlike walk, stepping lightly and looking down at the stones. She had wanted to be an opera singer like Mimi Coertse. She jangles her bracelets nervously on her freckled arms and flashes her black nails.

Ann, who was always blind and deaf to ordinary things but understood all the extraordinary ones, including our dreams, and who never cared for flowers, whispers to us, reminding us how we stamped our feet at Miss Nieven's Pekingese, Puck, and gave him an occasional kick to make him snarl, as he sat guarding Miss Nieven's door.

Fuzzie stares at us with apprehension from her close-set eyes and says that she has forgotten so many things. Her silver bracelets jangle as she flutters her fingers to convey them.

Two small black boys ride a skateboard up and down the path that goes to the pool. "You wouldn't have seen that before," the woman in the black shantung suit says, smiling at them. As she does so, we see her large, white teeth and shiny gums, and we recall the young girl we have carried in our minds through the years. We can bring her forth, tall and athletic, with her thin, hay-colored hair: Di Radfield, our captain.

We are the best of friends

MISS NIEVEN EMERGES from her room to lurch toward us like a ship on a rough sea. Her face is a web of wrinkles, her thin hair, punished with pins into a tiny bun. She leans on her cane. Called Sunny despite her olive complexion and her melancholy mien, she has more fine hairs than ever growing from the wart on her chin. She presses our hands and offers us her pale cheek.

Unlike us, she does not shy away from speaking of Fiamma. "A perfectly oval face," she says, recalling Fiamma's beauty.

We do not know what to say. Only Meg, dark-haired and Asian-eyed and herself a beauty, nods an assent, as the shadow from her leghorn hat shifts on her cheek. She is still straight and slender and pale. She did not go on to university but married young. Now she moves her hands smoothly in the air. She still has the mask of her soft, dark hair, her heavy lips, and the odd, empty expression in her dark eyes, which give no inkling of her thoughts.

In the shadows of the wisteria-covered veranda, Miss Nieven says, "There she was, lingering languidly outside Miss G's door." Her wrinkled face goes distant and tight. Our presence has stirred her memory. She surveys us blindly and says, "You were such a close-knit team, were you not? Devoted to one another. I was certain the thirteen of you would remain the best of friends."

Sheila, who always tried hard and has surely read the phrase in a book, says, "As close as a hand in a glove." We raise our eyebrows slightly, and we are all tempted to contradict her. In an instant she has touched on the reason we have been avoiding one another for so long.

One of us offers Miss Nieven a chair, and she settles down into the shadow in her mauve dress and amber beads, her back still stiff and straight. She has an M.A. from Oxford and had taught at a girls' school in India. She sat all day in her shaded study, guarded by her gray Pekingese, and made up programs for our activities: classes, prep, music lessons, ballet, riding, sport, and baths. When she made a mistake, she erased her small, penciled letters with her pink, oblong rubber. She wrote her sermons for chapel on Sunday: God of the Rushing Wind, of the Tumbling Waters, of the Mighty Mountains. Her favorite hymn was "Mine eyes have seen the glory of the coming of the Lord/ He is trampling out the vintage where the grapes of wrath are stored."

Miss Nieven rests her hands on her cane, tilts her head back blindly, looking as though she were talking to God, and says in her liquid, wobbly voice, "You were mostly in the water, rain or shine. We never had such a team. We were so proud of you — much prouder, I am afraid, than of our matriculation results that year." She laughs and waves a hand as thin as rice paper in the air.

Miss Nieven believed ambition was not seemly for Christian girls, for the meek should inherit the earth. She pauses, and we are afraid she has lost the direction of her discourse. Meg, who got a third-class matriculation, slips a cushion behind her back. Bobby Joe brings her a footstool. Miss Nieven lifts her arthritic legs one by one with difficulty, fusses with her skirt, and leans her cane against the chair. She opens her arms and exclaims, "The judges were always presenting those trophies to you. There you were, Di, your arms filled with trophies." Miss Nieven's voice has a raspy sound.

"We even beat Kingsmead," Di says, her pebble blue eyes

turning bright as she remembers our many triumphs. She coughs her smoker's cough and turns her head to the light. Her swollen face has a look of ill health. Her long, blond hair is cropped short and dyed copper. She still presents herself as if she had certain rights. She has to be taken into account in her black shantung suit with the padded shoulders and the large, unicorn-shaped diamond pin on the lapel. She has rubbed some dark rouge on her cheeks, and it makes her look much older — hard in a deathly and impressive way. Her once-slender body has run to fat, though she still has her broad swimmer's shoulders.

Miss Nieven says, "I used to like to watch you. If I saw one, I always knew where to find the others. It was almost a sunny dance, perfectly choreographed, a lovely garland of girls! You reminded me of that Matisse painting, you know the one I mean, with the blue background and all the pink figures holding hands, rising lightly into the air. There you were, swallow-diving from the high board in your black racing costumes, doing double back flips, one after another. Up, up you went into the air, light as light can be. I can almost hear the splash. You were so full of energy, enthusiasm, and life!"

No one cries out, "A dance? You call all those furtive, passionate writhings a dance?"

No one speaks of Fiamma's swallow-diving, opening her arms wide on the sky and earth, while Miss G gazes raptly up at her.

Di, who has dared to smoke, now stubs out her half-finished Craven "A" with its crimson smudge, pressing down hard, crushing it out with a spark of her old, uncontrolled temper. It lies smoldering in the dark earth around the potted palm next to the bench, while she crosses her arms, scowling.

Miss Nieven says, "And loyal, so loyal to one another! Always owning up, taking the blame. Diligent, too, and not only at swimming. I remember you, Ann, getting up before daybreak to help Fiamma with her Afrikaans, whispering to her in the window seat."

Ann Lindt, our vice captain, still sallow and thin, stands alone near the parapet, removes her thick glasses, and wipes her small, protuberant, pink-rimmed eyes. She laughs nasally and moves closer into the circle of women around Miss Nieven. Ann says in her pinched, secretive voice, "Fiamma was the best friend I ever had." Di looks at her askance and wipes the trace of crimson from her teeth with her tongue. There is a moment of silence.

Miss Nieven gazes blindly across the damp lawn and says, "Sometimes I think she is still out there and will come gliding across the lawn in her turned-down panama hat."

Sheila's cheeks flush as she says, "If she had to go off, it should rather have been to someplace grand. I can see her married to a handsome Milanese with lots of children, wearing a cloche hat, living in a grand house by a lake like the one she used to tell us about."

Miss Nieven turns toward the sound of Sheila's voice. "You were always making things up. I remember one of your Latin translations, which started out *In sylva,* which you translated "in heaven," and you went on to write of spirits wandering around the Elysian Fields."

No one says anything, but we all look at Sheila and remember how she used to make up long stories in the dark of the dormitory. We would fall asleep to the sound of her voice telling tales of Zulus with skin as pale as lilies or Chinese girls with blue eyes and fair hair. All her stories came to the same dramatic finale: violent death, whole families wiped out by Zulu impis or left to be eaten alive by red ants in a dry donga.

Why did Miss Nieven bring us back?

"YOU FIND THE SCHOOL much changed?" Miss Nieven asks. We evade her eyes and deflect her question. Ann opens up her small handbag and hunts inside, dipping her head and exposing the gray roots of her hair.

Ann had come to our school on a scholarship and had never swum in anything but the brown water of a ditch. She has married a rich black politician and lives in Harare, where she teaches political science at the university. She is one of the richest of us now and wears large corals around her thick neck and a square blue-white on her finger but still looks poor in her crumpled tartan with the big pin and her short-sleeved white shirt. No one asks her if it was Miss Nieven's letter, on the school's pale blue stationery with the dark blue crest at the head, which obliged her to come back to the school she disliked. No one mentions the contents of the letter that has brought us all back.

Miss Nieven says, "Tomorrow you must walk back to the river and visit the graves. Nothing has changed there — so far — but they may have to be dug up completely, as I told you in my letter." She leans her head back against the chair in a thin beam of light, as if overcome by the weight of it all. She stares blindly across the terraced lawns at what is left of the wild veld. She has suffered recently from fainting fits and for weeks has hardly ventured out of her room.

She sips water, pants, hauls herself up, and leans on Meg's arm. She makes an effort to straighten her back. She says that for this school to continue, it needs our help. Of course, it has been in difficulties before: there was all that trouble over Fiamma, she reminds us, blinking her small eyes blankly.

For a moment we think she has lost the thread of her thought. But she puts one hand to her flat, spinster breast, clutches at her amber beads, and says she thinks of our school as one of those monasteries that kept learning alive in the Dark Ages. There are few such places left, where the flames of Christian values, of love and learning, are kept alive. Half the student body comes here from farms with nothing: no money for books or even uniforms. They are beating at the gates.

However generous we may have been in the past, the school now needs our help more than ever. Without it a precious part of our past will be sacrificed. "The next thing you know they'll let a developer bulldoze those graves and turn up those bones." We look at one another, our faces pale.

It is, after all, a splendid summer evening, and the light is dazzling. There is no longer any hint of a storm. The sun, a lambent gold, is sinking beneath the horizon. Beneath it our old school grounds are disappearing into the twilight. The wind has dropped again. The air is sweet with honeysuckle, jasmine, and orange peel. The lawns are incandescent with heat and sheen. The red-hot pokers blaze. The dahlias smolder darkly. We stand and stare in silence. Only Ann is unimpressed. She turns sidewise to the lawns, cranes forward, and shortsightedly studies our faces, carefully. She is muttering some obscure line of poetry: *"Les deserts tartares s'eclairent."*

Miss Nieven moves toward Di and takes Di's gloved hands in hers, saying, "I am so glad you found the strength in your heart to come back." Then she turns, grasps her shiny black cane with the head in a shape of a bird, and totters through the door into the shadows. We hear the tap of her cane, as we stand, gazing into the distance across the veld toward the river.

PART TWO

DISTANCE

→>–<←

How we first heard about Fiamma

WE WERE THIRTEEN and fourteen years old. Meg, who
had been held back because she took a little longer to
learn, and Pamela Richter, the thin girl who always got less than
10 percent in maths, might have been fifteen. Sheila and the
Trevelyan twins were probably still twelve.

Most of us had been confirmed in our white Sunday dresses
and panama hats, because Miss Nieven had said this was not a
fashion show. We had made our first and last confessions.
Sheila had confessed to reading banned books but said she was
not sorry, because they told you the truth about life, and burst
into tears. Ann had told her to stop showing off. Most of us had
had our periods for the first time by then and spent much of
our time peering anxiously at the backs of our tunics, afraid we
might find a dark stain spreading shamefully there.

From the dusty teacher's platform, Miss Lacey, our English
teacher, was saying something about the arrival of a new girl,
Fiamma Coronna. We were probably in the second year of the
senior school. We were all in the classroom, sitting two-by-two
at our wide wooden desks with the tops that lifted to store our
books and our comics, and holes cut out to hold the inkwells.

Ann, who came first at maths, Latin, English, French, history, and backstroke — everything except science, music, recitation, ballet, and gym — was sitting in the front row beside another brainy girl who never made the swimming team. Ann was the only one who read the *Manchester Guardian*, which was sent to us from England on special, thin airmail paper and got pinned to the bulletin board, where it was flapping about in the cold morning air that came in through the open windows. She was wearing the thick glasses she had to wear because she was always reading. She read books by Winston Churchill, who was attacked in an armored train in the Boer War. She sat in the window seat in the early morning before we got up, reading his *Great Contemporaries* and looking up all the words she did not know, like *internecine* and *belligerent.* It was Ann who had asked Miss Nieven why the natives did not have the vote. Miss Nieven had said that democracy took a long time to develop.

Di, who could turn fifty cartwheels on the lawn and do pirouettes all around the assembly hall platform and was first at ballet and gym, was rocking on her chair in the back of the classroom, stretching her long legs. Beside her was Meg, who was reading comic books beneath her desk. Mary Skeen was best at science; she sprawled beside Pamela, who was not good at anything then but later took a First at sex. Fuzzie was first at music and recitation. She sat, peering out the window, next to Sheila in the gold glare of the winter sun. Fuzzie had a lovely voice for both singing and speaking. Miss Lacey often made her recite "Ozymandias" by Shelley at the end of class in order to curb any excessive ambition, not considered seemly for Christian girls. "Look on my Works, ye Mighty, and despair," Fuzzie would say, stretching out her fat, freckled arms and lifting her hands toward us, imploringly. Ann, who knew much poetry by heart, was tone-deaf. The Trevelyan twins, who were orphans, sat side-by-side in the middle of the classroom and were, like her, on scholarship. Miss Nieven said money had no importance and should not be mentioned in polite company. *On ne parle pas de l'argent*, she said then, in the days when the school had money.

Miss Lacey was saying, "May I have your attention, *please*, girls. I am trying to tell you that a new girl is coming all the way from Italy to our school, after the holidays. I want you to welcome her on her arrival. Girls, are you listening to me?"

It is almost certain we were not listening when Miss Lacey told us about the exceptional circumstances — something about a business trip — under which Fiamma was to arrive. We rarely listened. We had difficulty just keeping still. We bit our nails, the skin around our nails, the ends of our pens, the ends of pencils; we sucked our plaits and sometimes even smooth stones; we craned our necks to check for period stains; we scratched, picked, and peeled, at our scabs, our teeth, and our noses. Bobby Joe was presently busy surreptitiously wiping what she had discovered in her snub nose onto the bottom of her desk.

The gold glare of the winter light was coming in slantwise through the north-facing windows. We were sitting in our long-sleeved winter shirts and brown cardigans and striped ties, our breath misty in the early morning air, and muttering about it being worse than *Jane Eyre* in our unheated classroom. The highveld winter mornings were bitter cold, but by midday we would tie our cardigans around our waists, roll up our long sleeves, and lounge on the dry grass in the strong sun. Heating was not considered necessary where the winters were short and the summers long.

"Now I want you to be particularly nice to this new girl, who is coming from such a distance, from another country, another . . . background." Miss Lacey's voice rose in a vain attempt to persuade.

She knew that we were not nice to new girls, wherever they came from. We teased, tormented, and tortured them. We made them eat bitter aloe or swallow something nasty like cod-liver oil, or we gave them the black spot, which was supposed to frighten them, but, because most of them had never read *Treasure Island* and therefore did not know that if someone gave you the black spot it meant you were about to die, they only looked at us blankly.

Sheila told Bobby Joe, when she was a new girl, to put her towhead in the toilet and flush. She refused. "You have to," Sheila said, looking surprised, but Bobby Joe just walked away. Lizzie Turner broke Pamela's doll furniture for no reason at all when she was ten years old.

We were nasty to all new girls, especially foreigners. We were proud of our new country's independence, even if our mothers still called England home; after all, they had never been there. There was a new girl from England, pasty and plump, whom we called a killer. We made a circle around her and chanted, "You killed Joan of Arc." There was an American, Ramona Landsberger, whom we all called Ramooona Hamburger, imitating the way she answered all questions with a drawl, while she spat on her big, red mosquito bites. She did not stay long. The mosquitoes were too much for her. Africa was too much for her; we were too much for her.

We thought of all foreigners as "drips," whose soft feet made them unable to walk barefooted, as we could, across the hot, hard ground. We were sure they would get lost in the veld or fall into a deep donga or eat poisonous berries and die.

Miss Lacey was even older than Miss Nieven. She had blue-white hair and violet-blue eyes and wrinkled skin. She had told us that in her youth, at Oxford, Yeats had fallen in love with her violet-blue eyes. She was always quoting him, particularly his poem "When you are old and gray and full of sleep."

She was not quoting him this morning but informing us in hushed tones that Fiamma was actually a real princess. She told us that Fiamma was from an old, aristocratic Italian family, from the lake district not far from Milan. Her father owned great tracts of land, a large villa on the edge of a beautiful blue lake, famous paintings, rare jewels, a huge fortune. He was himself a prince, she went on, in her breathless way.

No one knew exactly why Fiamma's father had chosen this particular school, so far away from home, but Miss Lacey presumed he had his reasons; perhaps he had come across it in his travels, while searching for something else he wanted.

We shifted about and pulled at our socks and flared our eyebrows and sucked in our cheeks and goggled in mock amazement and awe. Di shrugged her broad shoulders and lifted the top of her desk as though she were looking for a book and mumbled, "So what" to Meg, who grinned. Ann, who never missed anything, turned around and gave Di her twisted smile. Pamela snickered.

We did not like aristocrats.

Naturally, being Italian, Fiamma was Roman Catholic, Miss Lacey went on, but she would attend religious services with the rest of us. She begged us to be gentle with her and to be mindful of her background. She said Fiamma had what she called a breathing disorder. Miss Lacey knew so much about Yeats, but little about young girls.

On the subject of R.C.'s

WE STOOD on the dry lawn during break, the sun warming our shoulders. We sipped hot tea from tin mugs and ate what we called squashed flies and stubbed the square toes of our lace-up shoes in the red sand. Bobby Joe picked her nose and maintained that the Pope kept all his old jewels locked up in vaults in the Vatican, while everyone else starved. Di told us her mother said Catholic nuns buried their babies in the backs of convent gardens. Sheila said her aunt told her those nuns were walled up in cellars when they sinned.

Meg, who was an R.C. herself, looked as if she were going to cry. She said she had never heard of such things, and she was sure no Catholics would do them, and anyway, what did being walled up alive mean?

"If you have done something really bad like having sex, they build a wall around you and leave you in there all alone in the dark to die, slowly, standing up. You can't even sit down to die," Sheila said, enjoying the drama of it all.

"They do that?" Meg's heavy lips trembled.

Fuzzie said, "Don't worry, they won't do that to you, Meg, even if you are an R.C., because you're beautiful and good as gold."

"She's not that good," Ann whispered to Sheila.

On Meg's bedside table she kept the photo of her mother and father with their five girls. The girls were all in faded dresses, and they seemed almost identical, sitting or kneeling on the ground, with their flat, pansy faces uplifted, showing off their slanting eyes and their heavy lips and their dark curls. All the girls were smiling, except for the youngest, who would die young of scarlet fever and was very nearsighted and did not seem to be aware that the photo was being taken, because her eyes were closed.

From the side of her thin mouth Ann whispered to Sheila that Meg's Catholic parents were not as perfect as Meg thought they were. Meg had confessed to her in a moment of confidence — Ann was good at getting our confidences with her probing questions, and Meg was no match for her — that her father beat his five girls once a week. He beat them with a sjambok out on the veranda, leaning over the back of a chair. They were beaten both for the sins they confessed and for the ones they did not.

Bobby Jean, who had been in a convent school, said Catholics were always trying to convert you in order to keep your soul from rotting in hell for eternity.

Lizzie said her mother said Protestants were rational and educated and kept their places of worship tastefully bare, whereas R.C.'s were superstitious and ignorant; they resorted to beads and candles and ghastly pictures of Christ, bleeding, with thorns around his head and nails in his hands.

We had all learned about Bloody Mary in history and how she killed so many Protestants because they wouldn't convert. We had all read a poem by the greatest poet in the English language, a poet who was even greater than Yeats, according to Miss Lacey, in which he asks God to avenge the saints slaughtered by the R.C.'s.

Perhaps Fiamma had seen some slaughtered, and that was why they had sent her away from her lovely villa, which was near a blue lake and mountains, Di suggested.

"We better watch out, the Catholic princess might want to slaughter some of us," Bobby Joe said.

It was then that Ann had one of her blinding revelations. She whispered to Sheila, "Miss G is going to like this new girl, you wait and see." She saw it in a flash.

What are cracks?

> We held our breath, we shut our eyes,
> We felt our heads spin.
> Our souls escaped into the skies,
> We heard a frightful din.
>
> In the dark we saw diamonds;
> Miss G sallied down the aisle.
> She touched us with her hands
> And bore us aloft, awhile.

MISS G WAS our crack. When you had a crack you saw things more clearly: the thick dark of the shadows and the transparence of the oak leaves in the light and the soft glow of the pink magnolia petals against their waxy leaves. You wanted to lie down alone in the dark in the music room and listen to Rachmaninoff and to the summer rains rushing hard down the gutters. You left notes for your crack in her mug next to her toothbrush on the shelf in the bathroom. If you accidentally brushed up against your crack and felt her boosie, you nearly fainted.

We all knew how to make ourselves faint. The teachers did not know we made ourselves do it, though they suspected we did. They even had a doctor brought in to examine us, but he said there was nothing wrong with us. He said he had never seen such a healthy group of growing girls. We did look healthy.

Our skins were gold with all the sunshine, and our hair and teeth looked very white in contrast. Weekdays in the summer term we wore short-sleeved white blouses with round collars and brown tunics with their big *R*'s embroidered on our chests and our long brown socks. Our tunics were worn four inches from the ground, measured kneeling, so you could see our knobby knees. In winter we wore long-sleeved blouses and ties.

We took turns fainting in chapel. Before communion, while we were on our knees and had not had any breakfast, we breathed hard a few times and then held our breath and closed our eyes. We sweated and started to see diamonds in the dark. We felt ourselves rush out of ourselves, out and out. Then we came back to the squelch of Miss G's crepe-soled boots as she strode along the blue-carpeted aisle to rescue us. She made us put our heads down between our knees, and then she lifted us up and squeezed our arms.

We leaned against her as we went down the aisle and felt her breath on our cheeks and the soft swell of her boosie. Our hearts fluttered, and we saw the light streaming in aslant through the narrow, stained-glass windows: red and blue and yellow like a rainbow.

Miss G led us out into the cool of the garden. We sat on the whitewashed wall under the loquat tree in our white Sunday dresses and undid the mother-of-pearl buttons at our necks. Miss G sat on the wall beside us and smoked a cigarette, holding it under her hand, so Miss Nieven would not notice if she came upon her suddenly. When Miss G told us to, we took off our panama hats and set them down on the wall. Then we leaned our heads against her shoulder. We got to sit there under the cool, dark leaves of the loquat tree and feel the breeze lift the hems of our tunics very gently and watch Miss G blow smoke rings, until she asked if we felt all right now. Her voice was deep and a little hoarse, like a man's.

Why Miss G called us to her room

> She called us to her room at night,
> She made us drunk on wine.
> We searched the truth with all our might;
> For her we write these lines.

IN OUR FLANNEL pajamas and plaid dressing gowns and flat leather slippers we huddled in Miss G's doorway and halfway down the long corridor, trembling and whispering. Why had Miss G summoned the twelve of us? She had never done so before this evening.

We were all whispering, looking at the faded reprints of Degas's ballet paintings, and waiting until she finished her conversation. We could hear her speaking and laughing on the telephone. To overhear her conversation better, Sheila, who was nosy, tried to get near the door. We gathered she was talking to the witty Mrs. Willis, the science teacher, who was her intimate friend at that time. Later Mrs. Willis became her enemy. Her best friends often became her enemies, because they betrayed her and took advantage of her great generosity, she said.

She was generous in many ways. Bobby Joe told us how Miss G sat by her bed in the sanatorium — a small, white building, set among blood red hibiscus bushes, where we were sent when we were ill — when she had the chicken pox. Bobby Joe forgot her itching while Miss G told her about a man she had fallen in love with when she was nursing in Wales during the war. She massaged his privates for him. Bobby Joe rubbed her small, strong hands together to show us what Miss G showed her.

Was it possible that Miss G had chosen us for her team? we wondered. We knew she banished girls whenever they disappointed her. Nor did they even know how they had disappointed her, or if they were to leave for good or simply to step aside for a while. Had she banished all the girls who had been there before us?

Fuzzie said that when she had gone to the san at the beginning of the term for her physical examination, the nurse had weighed her and measured her fluttering chest and slipped her cold, dry fingers under Fuzzie's warm, sticky armpits and held the ends of the tape measure together, asking her to inhale and measuring her again. "Miss G will want you," the nurse had told her, because she could expand nicely. Now she hummed a hopeful tune, wearing her vest under her plaid pajamas, and twisted her tight red curls around her finger. Her father was a musician and spoke of the four B's: Beethoven, Bach, Brahms, and Burls.

Expanding nicely was not the only reason Miss G chose girls for her team, Ann muttered mysteriously from over her shoulder, while standing on tiptoe to examine the Degas prints with a critical eye.

Meg said she thought Miss G chose the best-looking girls in the school for her swimming team. Sandra du Toit, who was already on the team, was certainly good-looking. And we, too, were good-looking, weren't we, Meg suggested, surveying our group with a benevolent eye.

We were good-looking. How could we not have been, growing up half-wild in fresh air, sunshine, and heat? Meg, of course, was particularly good-looking with her heavy, red lips, her slightly slanting, dark eyes, her slim waist, and her full bust. At fifteen, she looked lovely, even in her faded, shapeless pajamas.

Di flipped her fine, blond hair back from her face and stood on her long, slender legs, complaining to Meg about the wait. Ever since her father committed suicide in the bath, Di's thin lips dipped at the corners. She maintained Miss G chose girls who were rich and could contribute to the team fund. Some of us were rich: she had inherited her father's money. Fuzzie's father, who had inherited her mother's money when she died in a fire, had lots of money; Sheila's father, a timber baron, died of a heart attack and left all his money to her mother, who took to the bottle.

Ann, who was very poor, said Miss G probably chose anyone who could be useful to her. She helped Miss G with her correspondence and with the swimming-team quarterly, which told the school about its triumphs.

No one could think why Miss G had summoned the Trevelyan twins, who were not rich or pretty or useful, with their white hair sticking up on their heads like straw and their snub noses. They stood arm-in-arm, twisting about and putting their hands between their legs and wanting to go to the toilet. They were still horse-mad at twelve and tied their belts around Mary's waist and made her run around the garden, playing horsie and pretending to whip her. Perhaps Miss G chose them because they were orphans and had no one to turn to, Fuzzie whispered to Lizzie, the tall, elegant girl who spoke with an English accent.

Finally, Miss G covered the receiver with one hand and told us we might enter her room and find a perch. We filed in solemnly.

Miss G had acquired a room as large and as pleasant as Miss Nieven's. The bay windows were open to the evening light, which fell onto the silver jug of wet roses.

We could see through the big bay windows across the terraced lawns as far as the river on one side, and on the other up the green-gray hill as far as the pool. Unlike Miss Nieven, who kept her room shuttered and dim, Miss G always let in the sunlight. She believed it necessary to combat her skin malady, something mysterious with a Greek name, contracted as a child, that made her scratch from time to time.

Miss G sat in her wicker chair before her desk in her khaki jumpsuit and scratched at the bristles on the back of her neck in the evening light of her big, open room. She was slim and athletic. She seemed tall, although she was not as tall as Di. She had fine, tapered fingers and what she called good bone structure: high cheekbones and an aquiline nose. Her eyes were wide-spaced and large and as dark as night. They were mysteriously shaded by thick lashes and had a beautiful expression when she was carried away, which she often was. Her forehead was broad and generous, and her hair as glossy as a gypsy's. Her mouth had no droop but was firm and straight. Two deep lines ran from her nose to the corners of her lips. She was wearing what she always wore when she was not wearing her black bathing suit: her starched khaki jumpsuit, with a hand-embroidered belt, and her famous highly lacquered boots with crepe soles. Her clothing was always spotlessly clean and well-pressed and starched, and it made a whispering sound like the sea as she moved.

Sitting on the carpet with clammy, clenched hands and dry mouths, or perching on her bed like birds, we waited expectantly, gazing up at her, our name tags pricking our necks. There was no scratching or picking there; only stillness and docility. Miss G had bribed Mrs. Looney, our matron, with boxes of chocolates and nylon stockings to allow us to stay up at night in her room. She glowed, we thought, as though a halo surrounded her head. She spoke fast and impatiently, as though there were little time left.

"Shut the windows, Radfield," she ordered. She always called us by our surnames, as though we were boys.

We watched avidly as she took out two straw-covered demijohns of wine from her cupboard. She mixed the red and the white, pouring from both containers at once into a big white pitcher, with a glug-glug, something we had never seen anyone do before. She gave us glassful after glassful and told us to drink up. *In vino veritas,* she said. She liked to quote in Latin or from Shakespeare. She told us she was an autodidact, which meant that she had learned everything by herself.

She told us that whatever happened in her room was to remain a secret. We were not to tell anyone. We were not to fidget, not to ask questions, not to speak at all unless spoken to, and not to get up to go to the bathroom.

"I need your whole attention, if we are going to accomplish the great things I have in mind for you," she said, lighting a cigarette. When we had all solemnly promised to obey — we would have promised her anything — she informed us in a matter-of-fact tone that she simply needed some new blood. She was choosing twelve new girls for the team: us.

The whole room, with its bright yellows and blues and its large photos of Miss G's Welsh terrier, who died of some horrible disease, spun around. It was only afterward that we thought of the twelve girls whose places we had taken, especially Sandra, our head girl, a beauty, tall and brainy, slender and athletic, with red-gold hair, who had been Miss G's favorite, and who was suddenly banished.

She informed us that it was of no importance who was on her team, because she could teach anyone to swim. "I could teach a sheep to swim," she said scornfully, and we lowered our eyes and laughed sheepishly. We were certain she could do what she said.

She scratched her cheek, and we did the same. As she spoke, we moved our lips with her words. When she tapped her ash into the ashtray, we tapped our fingers. She held her handsome head high like a fist and pressed her broad shoulders back, soldier-like. We sat up and pressed back our shoulders.

Her hair was cropped so short you could see the bristles at the back of her neck, and she had burned her skin dark that summer, the result, she had explained to us, of the reflected light from the snow on a recent skiing trip to her native Wales.

She said that we were not to be deluded that she had chosen us for our innate ability to swim, or for any other particular abilities we had; on the contrary, she maintained, she had chosen us randomly. Anyone else would have done just as well. She said she chose her swimmers by chance, that is, as a manifestation of God's will.

She told us, "What is important in learning to swim well, as it is in anything, is desire," and her black eyes flickered mysteriously. She told us we could do anything if we desired it enough. We liked the way she said *desire,* and we looked at one another and raised our eyebrows and smiled.

She said we could and should break all the absurd rules that governed our young lives; we were to flout convention. "You can do anything you want. The world is yours for the taking. Nothing is impossible for you, my girls. Live your lives to the full. Do you want to be absolutely free? Do you want to escape your suffering bodies? All you need is to desire it."

She told us to use our imaginations, to concentrate, to think of nothing else, if we wanted to win; that everything was part of the race. She advised us to keep our bodies fit at all times, to eat fruits and vegetables and whole-grain bread and keep ourselves light for the rest of our lives. She told us to swim in the morning, at night, constantly. "Discipline," she said, "not talent, is what counts." Potential was simply the willingness to learn what she had to teach. "Don't let men wreck your bodies or bend your minds; be just like them." Her grandmother gained just fourteen pounds when she was carrying her mother, who weighed seven at birth; her grandmother was riding a horse at eighty. "You can be strong and beautiful until the day you die. Aim high." She lifted her big, strong hands and shook them at the high molding, as we all looked up.

She told us to think of the water as our own true home, to learn to do without breath, without air; to be light. We sucked in our stomachs and straightened our backs. She told us not to make any unnecessary movements in the water, not to roll about or twist our shoulders or lift our heads too high, but to suck a little air fast from the sides of our mouths. She said not to make any splash, to slice silently through the water, to cut through it, to kill. "Swim out of rage," she ordered, "and for God."

She wanted us to know she was not a failed intellectual but an educated woman, perhaps more educated than our headmistress with her degree from Oxford. She encouraged all of us to read and promised to lend us books from her library, not the books on our school syllabus, not *The Story of an African Farm*, not *The Tempest* or *Jane Eyre*, but books covered with brown paper, written by writers of whom we had never heard: Lawrence, both D.H. and T.L. She told Ann to read her namesake, Ayn Rand.

We stared up at her, trying to follow what she was saying. We often had great difficulty following her, because she spoke so fast and with so many long words and unusual expressions. "If you can't bedazzle them with brilliance, baffle them with bullshit," she said. Miss Lacey told us she was vulgar, having spent some time in America and picked up certain expressions there, but we knew Miss Lacey was jealous because she was old and washed out. We thought Miss G expressed herself brilliantly. If we could only understand her, we could learn the secret of life.

She went on in her mellifluous Welsh voice. She told us both that we were a worthless bunch who would never amount to anything and that we could be the best swimmers anywhere, with our names inscribed in history. She repeated our names. Radfield, Radfield, Miss G said, shaking her head. She used alliteration. She called Di, "Reckless Radfield," and Fuzzie, "Burls the Bear," because she was plump and awkward. Ann was "Logical Lindt" and Meg was "Darling Donovan," because she was beautiful and good and was always helping the little girls who came crying to her about their troubles. Mary Skeen was "Sweet Skeen," because she was placid and good-natured, and Lizzie was "Lucky Lizzie," because she got to spend the holidays in England with her father.

Miss G spoke of the importance of honor. She told us about Brutus: that the good of the team should triumph over the good of the individual. She told us that the means justified the end, which was to win and win again.

She spoke of truth and freedom from repression. She said the essential was to look into your heart honestly and to know the truth about yourself and, thus, about life. "If you find the truth within you, it will save you. If you ignore it, it will destroy you," she said. No one else would tell us the truth; we were brainwashed by a bunch of bland spinsters who knew nothing — or would tell us nothing — about life, who gave us a sugarcoated version of the truth. She imitated Miss Nieven sipping a cup of tea, lifting her pinkie in the air and talking about God the Rushing Wind, making us laugh with a delicious sense of complicity.

She said she would tell us about our headmistress, who, if she was not going mad, was at least more and more disorganized. She closed herself up in her room and did not respond to anyone for days. She was getting worse and worse. "All Sunny Nieven thinks of is taking your money. If I were your parents I would complain. She cannot even answer a letter anymore. And that's the truth."

"To thine own self be true, and it must follow, as the night the day, thou canst not then be false to any man," she recited. Now that we were on her team, we had to learn the art of telling the whole truth.

She would even tell us about herself, as an example. She told us her father was a dirt-poor Welsh miner, and a drunk, who made her kneel as a punishment, even when she had the curse, until she fainted; that he beat her mother, who made millinery, sitting up late at night sewing plastic cherries onto felt to supplement their small income; that she, Miss G, stole money from her grandmother's money box, which she kept under her bed, to buy her boat ticket to Africa.

"No inhibitions here! I will have no inhibitions here!" she said sternly. "Repression of libidinal urges only leads to aggression. Give me your secrets, girls, give me the dark depths of your hearts, and I will give you the light. Search your hearts, for the universe lies therein," and we searched and searched. "It is always more grubby than you think," she added, and we nodded our heads, knowing she was right. She said there were certain subjects we should get out of the way, so that we could go about our business. She knew what we were thinking.

"I know what you are thinking about, Darling Donovan, behind that angelic air," she said to Meg, making her squirm about and blush. "You are a quiet one, a regular little saint. But don't think I have not been watching you. You're interested in what everyone else your age is interested in, and it is not swimming."

She looked around the room for another victim. "And if our little saint is interested in it, just think how interested Reckless Radfield must be! Ah, Radfield, you are entirely honorable and good, but you are the most dangerous of all. Isn't she now? She is a sensualist. Are you not? I can see it from the way you throw yourself into the water, from the way you run across the veld, from the way you look at Meg." Di dared to look back at Miss G without blinking.

"And as for Logical Lindt, don't think you fool me either, my dear. You are far too clever for your own good," she intoned, shaking her head. "Your nose may be in a book for the moment, but you're just like the rest."

She proceeded to tell us in detail about the miracle of a man's erection. "Observe them as they swell in their bathing suits when they come near you." We giggled and smirked and imagined men's mysterious parts swelling like sunflowers in the warm light of our bodies. We were transformed into snake charmers, magicians. As the light faded and night fell, she advised us to adopt the habit of clenching our pelvic muscles after we urinated to tighten them, so that they could give pleasure. "Our muscles are like our minds: we must exercise them again and again," she said, as we clenched and unclenched them. *Mens sana in corpore sano,* she quoted. She told us that we must always tell her when we had our periods.

By the time Fiamma arrived, all of us had had our periods for the first time. The hot weather out here makes us develop early, Miss G told us, but Fiamma, being an aristocrat with blue blood, would do so more slowly.

The game of truth

THE MOON CAST its pale light in the long, narrow room as we sat on the floor in a circle whispering. Ann sat on the sidelines and called out "Stop," and Meg's hand was found at the bottom of the pile, so she had to answer the question.

It was Sheila who devised the game. Always one who tried hard, she suggested we practice telling the truth in the dormitory at night, as Miss G had suggested.

We all put our hands one on top of the other to make a pile and then pulled them out one by one, starting from the bottom, playing truth. Someone sat on the sidelines and called out "Stop," and whoever had her hand at the bottom of the pile had to answer a question truthfully. The only one who escaped, because we never asked her to play, was Fiamma — that is, until the day she disappeared.

Ann asked Meg what was the worst thing she had ever done.

Meg had been taught by her Catholic mother and father to keep her mouth shut, to chest her cards, so she said she could think of nothing.

Ann said, "Oh, come on. Out with it."

Meg confessed to putting a hairpin up her winkie, and then covered her face with her hands in embarrassment.

"You did that!" Di gasped, pulling her lips down at the corners, as though she were about to be sick.

Meg now sat on the sidelines and got to ask Di the same question. That is how we found out that Di had actually allowed a boy to put his finger up hers.

"So you're not a virgin?" Ann asked her, impressed.

"Not strictly speaking, I suppose," Di said with a superior air, flashing her strong, white teeth and her rosy gums at us in the moonlight.

After that we followed her around like dogs for days.

When Fiamma first arrived

WE HAD STAKED out our territory, fought over the best beds in Kitchener, and were bouncing on them, when Bobby Joe spotted a car approaching in a cloud of red dust in the distance.

It was the beginning of the spring term and a long period of drought. The October rains had not come to signal the end of a dry winter. Instead the wind blew across the veld, carrying a fine red-clay dust into the classrooms and dormitories. It settled in a thin film over the basins and dresser tops and windowsills.

Dust was flying from the wheels of the dark green Porsche, which came to an abrupt halt under the oak trees. A man got out, trailed by a blond girl, her head drooping like a snowdrop in the early spring. We had never seen such a handsome and elegant man. He looked shiny, striding up the polished red steps between the sandstone lions, two at a time, followed by a servant carrying leather suitcases of different sizes.

Leaning far out the window, Bobby Joe told us the man looked like a fairy with golden eyes.

Miss Nieven, too, was there on the steps in the full glare of afternoon light. She had not greeted any of our parents on our arrival but remained within the thick walls of her cool study, making up programs, or writing in pencil about God for her Sunday sermon, erasing with her big pink rubber when she made a mistake. She had left the task of greeting newcomers to Matron, the least important member of the staff, who had stood with her cardboard-backed list and licked her fat finger to turn the pages, looking for our names through thick glasses and ticking them off one by one.

But for this latecomer Miss Nieven was standing on the front steps in the sun, waving her white lace handkerchief about in the air like someone in a book, the lavender wafting up to us as we hung out the windows. She was wearing her best mauve dress, the one she kept for chapel on Sundays, and she had even pinned a posy of wilting violets to her flat spinster bosom. Her thin voice rose in greeting: "Welcome, welcome," she shrilled, shaking the father's hand, as though she would never let it go.

He was nattily turned out, in tweeds, in exactly the light-colored shirt and pastel tie and shiny shoes that fashion, as we imagined it, prescribed. His dark, glossy hair was perfectly trimmed, and his pale face freshly shaved. Fuzzie maintained his lips had been lightly touched with rouge.

"Definitely a poofter," Bobby Joe concluded, leaning dangerously far out.

We watched him leave, loping down the steps two at a time. The blond girl followed and clung to him. He had to pry her loose, and long after he had gone, we saw her standing there, looking down the dusty driveway, lingering in the shade of the oak trees while the sun set in a rush of red. She was still out there when dark fell swiftly, and we could hear a dog howl with a wild, wolf-like sound. Then she turned her face toward the school and dragged herself slowly up the drive.

Miss Nieven, who had politely refrained from interfering in this parting, was there again with a big smile to usher Fiamma into our dormitory. Tugging at the hair that grew from the wart on her chin, she told us to be sure to make the new girl feel at home, and then stood there as though she wanted to say more. We felt she would have liked to stay all evening to make sure we were kind.

Fiamma came into Kitchener followed by the servant carrying all her suitcases. The moment she entered the room, our eyes turned to her, as though there were something magical about her appearance. She stood there, blinking her dark eyelashes, the tears still on her cheeks, her long neck delicate but not frail, and her oval face tipped to one side. She looked as though she had just risen, naked out of the sea, and stepped into a shell, like the lady we had seen in the painting in art class. We tried to pay no attention to her, but we were all staring.

What drew our attention? Her eyes were unusually big, huge,

still disks, a strange shade of light blue and as clear as running water. Her expression, too, was not one we had ever seen. She did not seem to see us, or rather she seemed to see through us, as though she were looking into the distance or listening to some faint sound. She did not look either sad or happy, but removed, as though she had looked us all over, and found us wanting. It was the uncaring look of the outsider.

Her pale eyes and her pale plait, which lay on her shoulder, matched her milk white skin, which was that of a redhead. But her hair was not red, it was blond. Her nose was unusually straight and seemed pencil-thin at the tip.

The oval of her face struck us particularly. There was something soft and sweet about the curve of her cheek. We recalled it from the copies of Italian Renaissance paintings we had seen in art class. It was the smooth oval of the Florentine Madonnas, the face of the very young mother with her child. It made us feel lonely.

Fiamma turned to the servant who had brought in the leather suitcases, hatboxes, and vanity cases, all initialed, with combination locks and first-class tickets flying. "Thank you so much for your kindness," she said to him, and then, speaking to us in the same clipped English tone, she added, "Fiamma Coronna. Good evening," though no one had asked her her name.

"Good evening, Your Royal Highness," Bobby Joe quipped from the end of the dormitory. Pamela stood up and curtsied, and we all giggled.

A tear ran down Fiamma's pale cheek. It was the only time we ever saw her weep. She did not even weep on the Sunday afternoon she disappeared, after we had played the game of truth.

Ann said, "This one is not going to be with us for long."

Why did our parents send us to this school?

We came here on slow trains from afar,
Traveling through veld day and night.
We followed the evening star.
To arrive at this lonely place in the moonlight.

THE ONLY KIND OF SNOW we had at Christmastime was made from cotton wool, and the holly was made of plastic. It was so hot we sweated when we ate the roast turkey and potatoes and gem squash, and when they flamed the Christmas pudding, the light outside was so bright you could hardly see the flame. The poem we read did not make much sense to us because April was not the cruelest month and bred nothing out of the dead land.

In those days our school was entirely surrounded by farmland. For miles around there was nothing but a few mangy cows, wattle trees, and pale mud huts, their skeletal frames visible in the blinding light. The dirt roads lay dry and white as shells in the sun. Sandy paths led across the veld to the river and the graves. An iron gate closed on the long driveway, lined with ancient oaks, that led up to the school.

No one was here except the girls and the teachers, who were elderly spinsters from England no longer able to find gainful employ in their home country, because of age or eccentricity or the commission of some minor misdemeanor. They clasped their hands to their hearts and looked across the veld to the distant horizon and longed for the lilac in May. The big girls lolled in the leather chairs in the common room and listened to Elvis singing "Hound Dog," and talked about boys. They slept over sums in the classrooms or whispered in the library, while they pretended to look up Latin verbs.

We were sent here as boarders at five or six, because there were no proper schools where we lived. We left our parents on distant farms or in small towns and traveled alone or in little groups for days on trains through wild country. We arrived exhausted and confused, stumbling through the long, narrow passageways, lit only by Matron's torch, and finding our beds among strange sleeping girls. The sheets smelled damp and funny. We lay awake, listening to the clashing of the palm fronds in the dry wind.

We cried for our mothers until Matron came to us in her dressing gown with her gray plait over her shoulder, trying to bring comfort. But she did not smell of flowers like our mothers. She did not feel like them. Her bosoms dangled slackly down to her thick waist under her rough dressing gown with the twisted red-and-white twill. Her hair was not silky like our mothers' — if we dared to touch her limp braid at all. She clucked her tongue at us. She told us our noise would only wake the others. When we got to the hiccupy stage, she took our temperatures with the thermometer she took from a small glass of Dettol with a snap of her wrist. Her name was Mrs. Looney, and we thought she was, too.

Night after night we wept for our mothers. If we went on wailing for too long and woke the other girls, Mrs. Looney took us to the spare bed in her small, stuffy room. We lay awake in the dark, sniffing and hiccuping and listening to her stertorous breathing. We stared up at the sky and tried to find the stars that looked down on our homes, remembering where we ate cold sausages with our sisters, sitting up in the bay window after church on Sunday, looking over the lawns, watching the big white tickbirds picking at the dirt.

We saw our mothers standing in the open window. They came to us in the half dark, their soft breaths on our cheeks, as they sang us familiar songs: "Underneath the budding chestnut trees." They were slipping their rings onto our fingers and toes;

they were rocking us on their knees and reciting rhymes: "She shall have music wherever she goes."

Mornings we saw their faces as we tried to untangle the knots in our hair, or as we lay in the big bath with the claws for feet. We heard their voices coming from down the corridor; they would bring us the cakes of soap we had forgotten in the dormitory. They sat on the branches beside us in the loquat trees and tickled our necks with leaves. We thought we heard them calling our names, and we ran down into the bamboo at the end of the garden, catching glimpses of them parting the bamboo and stepping toward us in green silk dresses, but it was only the cry of a sparrow hawk or the wind in the leaves.

We made up imaginary friends. Sheila's was called Margaret. Margaret came with her to the toilet to talk to her when she had to make number two or ran beside her when she had to run around the hockey field, her breath rasping in her chest.

We felt ourselves spin out into the darkness, round and round, like a leaf on water.

On Miss G's team

WE WERE ALL WINNERS and losers at different times, and our status on the team waxed and waned. We were willing to do anything to improve our precarious positions. We were constantly terrified Miss G might dismiss us, cast us out into the darkness of purgatory, lump us with the girls who were not on the team and who hardly seemed to exist at all.

Once on the team, we rarely mixed with the other girls in our class or any of the other classes. They had become boring. They seemed to have been washed away, to have left the school and vanished. Even Sandra du Toit, our head girl that year, who was beautiful and brainy and good at games, but no longer on the swimming team, no longer mattered. The swimmers were the only ones who did, because they were the only ones who mattered to Miss G.

Besides, Miss G had always tried as much as possible to group her team members in one dormitory on the pretext that we would disturb the other girls by rising early for swim practice. She knew well that it was in the whispered conversations in the night that affinities were formed, that it was while sitting in the window seat, staring up at the garlands of stars hanging low and bright in the African sky, that confidences were exchanged.

We stood on the high board for Miss G, trembling with suspense, looking down at the light fragmented in the water, opening our arms on the air, plunging through it, splitting the surface of the water with hardly a splash, toes pointed to the sky.

We rose early to swim before assembly; we swam two hours after rest in the afternoon and again at dusk. We always had cramps in our toes. Our hair was always wet. Our hands were always damp and cold and our fingers crinkled. Our eyes were always bleary with chlorine, as we gazed dazedly down at our damp books. Our pillows were soaked when we lay our heads down to sleep.

Meg and Miss G

> Behind her dark head was the sun,
> As she leaned across and touched Meg's knee.
> She was marked forever as the one,
> Forever branded by Miss G.

THE SUN LAY in a diamond shape on the soft carpeted floor, filling the big tearoom. A glass vase stood in the window with mimosa branches spreading fan-like against the sky. Women leaned close, the flowers in their hats trembling. They whispered and sipped tea, their little fingers lifted in cream leather gloves. Waitresses wore black dresses and frilled white caps, which floated like boats on the backs of their heads. They pushed tea carts on wheels, piled high with wondrous cakes: éclairs and little tarts with whipped cream and big, ripe strawberries, the kind Meg adored and almost never got to eat, she told us later. Miss G bought her several of them — one with cream and strawberries — and several cups of tea poured from a shiny silver teapot with straight sides and a little matching pitcher of milk. She noticed how Miss G slipped several packets of sugar into her many pockets and patted them with satisfaction.

On Fridays we were allowed to go into town for doctors' or dentists' appointments. This Friday, Miss G had accompanied Meg when she had to go to the doctor for her severe period pains. After the visit to the doctor, she had taken Meg out for tea in a big department store in the center of town, a place where Meg had never been before.

Miss G leaned forward and asked Meg, who was stuffing cakes into her mouth, about her family. She was glad Miss G was asking her this and not, as she often did, something more difficult that she might not understand. "How on earth does your poor father cope with so many girls?" she wanted to know.

Meg took another quick bite of cake and a sip of tea before answering. She felt warm in the sunshine, and started to explain how she tried to help her father by doing as many of the household chores as she could, rising early to clean the floors. Then she remembered how Miss G had said that we should tell all the truth and bring the dark parts of our lives into the light, and though she was not quite sure what a dark part was or whether she had any to be brought into the light, she found herself revealing what she had never told anyone before.

She told her how her father beat her and her sisters, making them lean over a chair once a week out on the veranda so that he could beat them with a sjambok, one after the other; the worst part was watching. She could not stop herself from watching. She drew aside the muslin curtain at the window and watched her father beat her sisters, starting with the youngest girl, the delicate one, watching and listening to their desperate cries for mercy. She knew that her father knew she was watching, that he wanted her to watch — indeed, needed her to watch, and that he would beat her harder than all the rest because she had been doing so, beat her until she lay unconscious on the floor.

When she stopped speaking, she waited, a little breathless and flushed, for Miss G to murmur words of sympathy or approbation for bringing forth into the light such a dark part of her life. She thought Miss G would pat her on the back and tell her how reckless and brave she had been, or perhaps even order a few more cakes as a reward, but Miss G did nothing of the sort. She leaned forward slightly and briefly placed her hand, lightly but unmistakably, on Meg's knee.

"There wasn't anything sexy about it," Meg told us, but it seemed to her that something enormous had happened. She had the strange but certain impression that Miss G was branding her as one of her own. Everything spun around her: the waitresses in black dresses, their little, frilled white caps, the shining silver teapot, the strawberries on the cream cakes, the yellow of the mimosa branches in the vase by the window, even the light in a diamond pattern on the carpet. Meg wanted to hold on to the moment like a precious gift, a jewel, something to be kept wrapped up forever in pink tissue paper.

How Fiamma made the swimming team

> For Fiamma she could skim across the water,
> As fast as can be,
> For she was a prince's daughter,
> And Miss G loved her most passionately.

MISS G TOLD US she was not entirely satisfied with her new team. She might choose some new members, or get rid of some of those she had already chosen. She was going to make the girls on the team race with the rest of the class. We could choose the stroke we liked and had to swim two lengths of the long pool. She told us to wait on the dry grass by the pool in our thin, black racing costumes, the spring sun burning our tender skin purple.

She liked to keep us waiting, for it enabled her to see who had real character and would stay the course. She said it was character, not talent, perseverance, not promise, that counted.

Fuzzie swatted at mosquitoes, which seemed drawn to her plump, bare legs and arms. Di tossed her long, thin hair impatiently. Lizzie practiced her crawl in the air, stretching her long, white arms. We rose up on our toes or crouched down on our heels with our elbows on our thighs and hands between our legs. We milled around, licking from the palms of our hands the powdered sugar we had obtained from Di.

Miss G called out the names of the whole class alphabetically and had us line up: "Allenby, Arkright, Bell, Burls, Fiamma Coronna . . . ," she called. Our legs felt watery, like the reflections of legs in water. We squirmed. We pulled the straps of our green plastic caps away from our chins. Color washed from the sky. Finally, she raised her black gun in the white air.

The water glittered; the sun blazed. We saw birds shoot up in the air and heard the crack of the gun. We flung ourselves across the water, crowding together. We splashed and kicked and crashed into one another, struggling breathlessly in a series of races, one after the other. When she saw that she was not winning, Sheila threw up her arms and sank down into the water, pretending to faint, so she would have to be dragged out.

The winners of each heat then swam a final one. Fiamma left all the rest of us behind after a few strokes. Miss G had her swim alone, timing her with her stopwatch, while we had to stand and look on. The spring sun was burning our cheeks, and the sweat was dripping into our dazzled eyes. We put up our hands to shade them, watching Fiamma flying back and forth across the surface, silvered by sun and spray.

Miss G stood in the shadows of the changing huts, her arms crossed, her wide lips trembling, and her yellow whistle dangling unused on her chest. The light in her dark face was strange and cast a glow. There was an expression of joy and pain at the same time.

She strode to the edge of the pool and leaned over to give Fiamma her broad hand and pull her out with one swift, strong movement, the water rushing from Fiamma's white skin like silver ribbons. She stood in the sun on the sides of her narrow feet on the hot concrete around the pool, gazing at us directly, as though it had been the easiest thing in the world.

"Hurry up and get her a towel," Miss G shouted imperiously. She draped it carefully around Fiamma like a royal cape and flung her arm around Fiamma's shoulders. She led her away, talking earnestly, bending her dark head toward Fiamma's blond one. They went together toward the changing huts, their shadows mingling in the dry grass.

What Fiamma liked about swimming

SITTING ON THE WOODEN bench in the changing room, where Miss G had left her after the tryouts, her thin, wet racing costume clinging to her narrow body and her pale plait lying on her shoulder, Fiamma lifted her inhaler and pumped to get her breath. She told us she did not want to be part of our team. "I don't want to swim for Miss G," she said.

"You don't?" Meg gasped in disbelief, watching her pump.

Fiamma suffered from a condition that made her use the inhaler. From time to time she placed it in her mouth and pumped on the soft brown bag. The other teachers said she had asthma and allowed her to climb out of the pool and lie down in the shade with her towel over her back or to sit on the bench and run her fingers through her blond, wavy hair, reading a book in gym in her bloomers, which showed off her slender legs, while we sweated and groaned on the hard floor, vaulting over the pommel horse or doing endless jumping jacks, sit-ups, and press-ups, which were supposed to combat any excessive interest in sex. We believed Fiamma was pretending most of the time, using her supposed illness to avoid whatever she wished to avoid.

"I like swimming fast. It feels like flying," she told us. She swam until she felt one with the water. She liked its mysterious sound in her ears — a sound like music, she said. She liked the way her mind floated free. She was never tired out swimming, except when she had her asthma attacks. On the contrary, swimming invigorated her. She was addicted to it, she said, it was like a need for air. If she could not swim she became restless, bored, edgy. Swimming was not a sport for her; it was where you could be who you really were. Besides, it was the only place where you could be on your own in this school. Fiamma said she found the lack of privacy unbearable.

We were not supposed to go off on our own. It was considered dangerous. We were not even allowed to lock our doors. The toilets and the small white cubicles where we washed for exactly ten minutes — baths were no longer allowed because of the drought — remained unlocked. We even took brief showers together in the bathroom under the stairs — Meg, Ann, and Di, all together, scorching themselves under the old shower that was impossible to regulate. Wherever we went, we heard the teachers' low voices and the high-pitched ones of girls. We were together day and night, eating, washing, learning our lessons, reading, sleeping, whispering in the dark, even going to the lavatory in the stalls where we could see feet and heads and talk to one another, while we strained and pushed. It would be unbearable here without the swimming, Fiamma said.

She told us she had no memory of learning to swim. Her father, who had been a championship swimmer himself, even swimming the channel, had thrown her into the water before she could walk. She kept a photo of him in his full-length swimsuit in a beaten-silver frame by her bed. His head was flung back, his dark, wet hair swept from his forehead. There was a towel slung around his neck. He appeared to be laughing.

She had no desire to compete in races, Fiamma said. In all her life she had never had to compete. She had grown up alone in her father's house with only an old servant for company. She had seen her mother and her half sister infrequently on visits to Milan, and neither of them could compete with her. Her father hated the one and refused to recognize the other, rarely mentioning her name.

Furthermore, she told us, she liked to swim because she had been found near the water, or so she was told by the old servant. He was a teller of tales. He was cleaning the changing huts near the lake, he said, when he heard cries. He was afraid some peasant had tried to drown a kitten, as they often did, weighing them with heavy stones and throwing them into the lake, where they would sink down into the dark of the soft silt of the lake bed. Instead, he found a newborn baby in a basket. "Like the story of Moses in the bulrushes. Only there was no massacre of babies, just a note from my mother in my shawl, which read, 'Returning that which belongs to you,'" she told us in her deadpan voice.

How Fiamma came to join the team anyway

THE LONG DESKS stretched all the way across the laboratory. There was a faint smell of smoke and methylated spirits in the dusty air. Ann was standing very straight and small in front of the class and succinctly and clearly explaining some experiment that no one else had understood when the laboratory door swung open abruptly, and Miss G put her dark head inside. She needed to see Fiamma urgently, Miss G said to Mrs. Willis, the science teacher.

Miss G had been Mrs. Willis's particular friend, but now she hated Miss G passionately. Mrs. Willis, the science teacher, had told us that the story about Miss G's parents was utter nonsense, that it was like something out of Dickens, and that Miss G's parents were very much middle-class and doted on Miss G and had sacrificed to send her to the best schools in Wales, where she continuously broke all the rules and was sent home.

Mrs. Willis maintained Miss G had been shut up in a mental asylum for a while, that she had been institutionalized, held in a straitjacket. Her parents died alone and unloved but respectably in an old-age home, according to Mrs. Willis.

Miss G had told us that Mrs. Willis was a lesbian. She had seen Mrs. Willis in the driveway making out with Miss Lacey, the English teacher whom Yeats had once loved.

Everyone said Mrs. Willis was very brilliant. She was sent down from Oxford because of some mysterious scandal, but she still received parcels of books with strange titles from England. Ann maintained Mrs. Willis read Marx and was probably a Communist, and Fuzzie that she was a spy, but Fuzzie always exaggerated. Di believed that Miss G was right, and that Mrs. Willis was a lesbian.

Whatever Mrs. Willis's sexual preference, she was always leaving us to cope on our own with our Bunsen burners, endangering our lives, while she disappeared into the science closet to have a quick drag on a cigarette. We were always blowing up our experiments, singeing our eyelashes, our eyebrows, while Mrs. Willis dragged on her cigarette. She wore a white coat without bothering to do up the bottom buttons, so that you could see her slim knees in her pale gray stockings. She was pacing before the blackboard, a piece of chalk in her hand, listening to Ann explain the experiment, while no one else except Mary listened, at the moment when Miss G put her head in the door to ask for Fiamma.

Mrs. Willis hissed at Miss G in her raspy, smoker's voice, "I am in the middle of a science lesson, if you don't mind," and gave her a furious look with her small, gray eyes. Miss G glanced over the rows of long desks that stretched from one side of the room to the other. Fiamma sat by the wall with her head down on the desk, apparently asleep.

Miss G said, "I don't think Fiamma will miss much of your science lesson. This won't take more than a minute. It's urgent." She told Fiamma to come with her. Fiamma lifted her head and looked up blankly, glancing from Mrs. Willis to Miss G, and blinked her big eyes. Then she shrugged her shoulders with her usual indifference and rose, yawning as she made for the door, almost knocking over a Bunsen burner as she went.

Fiamma was always careless in class. She wandered in late and forgot to bring the right books or dropped them on the floor while someone was reading aloud. She was always losing her pen and borrowing one from Sheila, who had several in preparation for her future career. Fiamma rarely bothered to answer questions, or when she did, answered the previous one. She always got up the moment we were dismissed, sauntering out without her books. She regularly fell asleep over her homework in the evening, her head in her arms. Yet the teachers would watch her, smiling fondly and indulgently, without ever scolding her.

Still, she could answer questions no one else could about history, and she surprised us with her knowledge of the ways of the world. She possessed odd information: she knew about Garibaldi and the Carbonari and Mazzini and about some old Italian king who had said, *"Avanti Savoia!"* She played the Moonlight Sonata so that we were moved to tears, but she did not care for it. When she recited Keats's "The Eve of Saint Agnes" at the drama competition, she forgot her lines halfway through, but the judge commended her on the sweetness and musicality of her voice.

Under the loquat tree at break we formed a circle around her and questioned her. She told us how Miss G had persuaded her to join our swimming team.

In her splendid, sunny room with the big photos of her dead Welsh terrier on the walls, Miss G told Fiamma to sit down in the comfortable armchair and offered her a glass of wine, which she declined. She asked Fiamma if she were happy at our school. Fiamma said she had not expected to be happy here, and hoped not to have to stay for more than a few months. Miss G knew it must be very lonely for Fiamma so far away from her home. She knew how Fiamma must feel, for she, too, was a foreigner, after all, and she, herself, was often lonely out here.

Fiamma said nothing. What was there to say, after all? Then Miss G asked if there was not something — any little thing — she could do to make Fiamma's stay more comfortable, to make her feel more at home. Fiamma said she thought for a while and then confessed that there was one thing she particularly missed.

And what was that? Miss G wanted to know, leaning forward eagerly, her elbows on her knees. Fiamma said it was her breakfasts: the crispy sweet rolls and coffee with steamed milk, brought to her in bed on a tray by the old servant. He always tapped the spoon against the cup to wake her, before he entered. Then he would throw up the shutters to let the sun stream in pools into the room.

"If you promise to swim for me, I will see what I can do," Miss G said, raising her eyebrows and wagging a finger at her, smiling, as Fiamma left the room.

In the long, narrow dining room with its odor of oranges and burned porridge, we cast hostile glances at Fiamma as the servant brought her special breakfast on a tray: sugarcoated white rolls and coffee with steamed milk, served on blue-and-white willow-pattern china. We whispered about Your Royal H —— as we shoveled the dark, lumpy porridge called maltabella into our mouths, washing it down with weak, milky tea from tin mugs that scalded our lips. Even Darling Donovan, who had such a sweet tooth, managed to complain that it was just too unfair.

Now our team had thirteen girls, not twelve. Inevitably, when we lined up double-file to walk to the bus, one of us would be left out. Inevitably, as best friends were formed, one of us would have to be rejected.

Was Ann Fiamma's best friend?

ANN DID NOT WANT to be Fiamma's friend, but she had little choice. No one else wanted to be her friend. No one invited her out on Sundays, when we were allowed to go home. No one invited her for half term. No one ever invited her, because of her small, protuberant eyes, her shiny forehead, and her stilted conversation: she could not chatter inconsequentially, as the rest of us did, but could only hold forth about the French Revolution and the Rights of Man.

"Your head's always in the clouds," Miss G told Ann, as they walked under the heavy leaves of the oak trees along the driveway to the bus. "You ought to think about more practical things, Lindt. For example, your skin. You ought to take care of it. Looks are more important than thoughts, you know. Why don't you ask Sister to give you some medicated soap for your blackheads, my dear," she suggested, looking at Ann's blighted nose and cheeks. "And, I feel obliged to tell you, your nails are not very clean, either, dear. Your fingers are always stained with ink, and you have a big blue bump on your writing finger from pressing too hard."

Miss G told her to pair off in the future with Fiamma. "Walk with her from now on, Lindt; it will do you good. Study her. Learn to put your shoulders back, as she does. Carry your head high. Imitate the way she carries herself. It will improve your prospects."

But Ann could not carry her head high, as Fiamma did, and though she brushed her hair as much as she could and rubbed her skin with Trushay, her hair remained dull and her big forehead shiny and bulbous as ever. She could not write a line that looked the way Fiamma's did, flowing in royal blue ink with rhythmic Italian curves.

Miss G wanted to make sure that Fiamma was never the thirteenth girl, the one rejected. She was determined to spare her any unhappiness. But she was punishing both of them, unwittingly, in throwing them together. She probably thought Ann and Fiamma would talk about books, never bothering to notice that they did not like the same ones.

Fiamma was always reading. Like all of us she read Keats and Wordsworth and Browning, but she also read Italian and French novels of which we had never heard. These, even Ann did not know.

Sitting in the long, narrow dining room in the glare of early morning light, after breakfast, digesting lumpy porridge, we listened hopefully as the prefect read out the names of girls who had received letters or parcels. We hoped for our names to be called, so we could walk up to the head table to pick up our items. Fiamma's name was called every day. So every day she sauntered through the crowded dining room to pick up the fat letters or parcels of dried fruit and cake and nuts from Italy; the chocolates called kisses in large boxes with many layers; the brown-paper parcels covered with stamps, which she opened after breakfast on the lawn, carelessly letting the paper fall to the ground; the piles of gold-embossed, leather-bound books in Italian or French in beautiful, rich colors with silk ribbons in them to mark her progress. She smelled their pages as though they were flowers.

What were the books about? we wanted to know. Fiamma told us Maupassant's story of the fat prostitute who is made to sleep with a Prussian, even though he is the enemy; Manzoni's story of the nun who is closed in the convent against her will; Dante's story of the visit to the underworld led by a slip of a girl. She shut the book with her finger between the pages and quoted the first verses of Dante's *Inferno* by heart in Italian in her singsong voice, when all most of us could quote were the lines we had been forced to learn as a punishment from "The Ancient Mariner": "Water, water, everywhere, nor any drop to drink."

Ann, whose mother and father were too busy on the farm to write and too poor to send parcels, borrowed her books from the library. She preferred history and philosophy and psychology, not poetry and novels, but she was obliged to ride on the bus beside Fiamma when we went to the swimming meets or on our rare visits to town. She was obliged to walk with her when we walked back to the bus, double-file. They walked side-by-side in uneasy silence. The role of the reject was left to Fuzzie, who was confused anyway.

Fiamma's visit to Ann's home

MISS G CALLED ANN to her room and suggested she invite Fiamma home for the short spring holidays. Apparently, Fiamma's father had come down with a bout of malaria during his visit to a game reserve and was in the hospital somewhere, delirious with fever. What could Ann say? she asked us. She knew it would be disastrous, but it was much worse than she had envisaged. To start with, there was the long, slow train ride together all the way to Salisbury, with Fiamma just sitting there, staring sulkily out the window at the veld and complaining about the heat, or reading obscure Italian novels, or writing endless letters to her father, lifting her slim, silver fountain pen to her lips and writing smoothly in royal blue ink.

At the small, hot station with the sun-blanched walls, Ann's mother and stepbrothers emerged from the shadows of the russet tin roof. Ann saw them through Fiamma's eyes: two louts with long khaki socks and short khaki shorts and thick, red necks and white eyelashes and small eyes. Ann suddenly found herself hating them passionately as they stepped forward onto the platform, blinking their sheeps' eyes stupidly in the sunshine.

From the moment Fiamma stepped delicately off the train into the sunlight, with the brim of her panama hat turned down to shade her white skin, and the lovely oval of her face tilted slightly to the side, and her long, blond plait on her shoulder, Ann could see that her stepbrothers had fallen in love with her. They were in love as they both reached for Fiamma's big leather suitcase at once. They were in love as they banged their thick heads together, laughing like idiots. They were in love as they squeezed their long legs and thick knees up to their chins, one on each side of her, in the back of the old, narrow Morris, which bumped over the dust strips all the way to the tobacco farm, where Ann's father kept losing his tobacco crops to the locusts and the heat and drought.

Worse still, Ann saw her mother, as well, through Fiamma's eyes. She had a maths degree from Oxford but had given it all up for love. She had married Ann's father, an impoverished farmer with sandy hair and freckles and these two big, ungainly boys from a previous marriage. Ann saw her mother standing there in the unforgiving sunlight, looking harassed and shabby, her shirt coming out of her drab, gray skirt, her unsupported breasts drooping, and her mousy hair caught back and hanging mournfully on her neck. Ann was ashamed of her shame.

For her amusement Fiamma was taken riding with Ann's mother, leaving Ann behind, for there were only two riding horses. When the horse stepped on a twig and startled a bird into rising suddenly in the air with a great flapping of wings and galloped off, she hung courageously on to its back and was praised for her excellent horsemanship. Ann's mother never praised Ann for anything, despite her consistently high marks. She took Ann's extraordinary brain for granted and always felt obliged to give the tastiest morsels of meat to the two big boys who were not hers.

She suggested the girls help her bake a cake. Fiamma lolled about the big farm kitchen, with its beams and thatched roof, striking interesting poses, one hand on her hip. She looked out the window at the chickens, clucking in the dusty sunlight, or she perched on the side of a table, swinging her slender legs slowly back and forth. When Ann's mother asked her to break an egg into the mixing bowl, she took the egg and held it delicately between her finger and thumb and lifted it up to the sunlight and considered it for a while, as though it might be something precious. Then she broke it on the stone floor, not in the blue-and-white-striped mixing bowl, and stood there, looking slightly surprised, while Ann was made to clean it up.

Fiamma strode off for a walk one morning, taking only the two big ridgeback dogs, a book of Italian poetry, and a bottle of water up the koppie. In those days leopards often came down from the hills to steal a sheep. When she did not come back by dusk, the whole family was in a state of anxiety. The two brothers rushed around, pulling at their hair and searching everywhere, as did Ann's father, when he came back up to the house from the land in the evening.

It was he who found Fiamma lying idly under a baobab tree, resting her head on its roots reading her book of Italian poetry. "You shouldn't have worried. The dogs would have looked after me," she said, when Ann asked her what on earth had made her stay out for so long.

Worst of all were the dinners, Ann told us later. Fiamma sat between Ann's brothers, wearing her lovely blond hair loose on her shoulders. It glowed in the kerosene lamplight, and her skin shimmered like milk, and her clear, blue eyes gleamed. Each time she lowered her lashes, the whole table seemed to tremble.

In the evenings she dressed herself up in the red silk kimono her father had brought her back from a business trip to Japan, all hand-embroidered with dragons and flowers. She wore little pointed silk slippers. Every time she reached across the table, as she did repeatedly, the sleeve of her kimono would fall away, revealing the way up her white arm to her budding bare bosom. The stepbrothers, and Ann's father as well, angled their necks to look.

On her last night, he opened a bottle of white wine, for the first time Ann could remember, and told Fiamma stories about his experiences in the war that he had never told Ann. He looked more handsome than ever to Ann with his sandy hair and freckles and his big, boyish grin. Looking at Fiamma closely, he said, "Those were the happiest days of my life," as Ann's mother pursed her lips into a thin line.

Swimming at midnight with Miss G

> Oh, Miss G, we will love you forever,
> For you we will swim night and day.
> Oh, Miss G, we will desert you never,
> For you we will fight in every way.

IN OUR DREAMS we heard Miss G calling us softly. She stood in the moonlight in the door of the dormitory. She made us get out of our beds in the white light of the moon. We rose, dazed, but in her surprising presence immediately awake and ready to follow. She said "Going swimming. Too hot to lie in bed."

The summer term had hardly begun, and already our hair stuck to our sweating foreheads, our pajamas to our backs. We stumbled about half asleep, looking for our swimming suits in the dark. Miss G told us not to be so absurd. We would not need swimming suits; we would swim in our birthday suits.

"Don't wake Mrs. Looney," Miss G said as we tiptoed down the neon-lit corridor past her door, leaning forward in an attempt to make ourselves small.

In the night-scented garden we huddled close. We whispered and giggled in the hot half darkness, following Miss G. She glanced behind with her dark, restless eyes. "Where's the new girl?" she asked, while Fiamma lingered languidly, staring up at the vast jewel tree of stars. Finally she spoke up. "Present," she said. She adopted the clipped accents of the English, though she had never been to England. She said "drawing room" for "lounge" and "sand shoes" for what we called "takkies." She did not end her sentences with "hey," as we did, and she never used the word "man" as a form of address.

"One finger on my back, Fiamma," Miss G commanded, as we climbed up the hill, going toward the pool in the pale light of the moon. Fiamma looked at Miss G for a moment, not understanding perhaps that Miss G would always have one of her girls pretend to push her up the hill with one finger to her back.

"Just one finger, to get me up the hill, dear," Miss G reiterated, and smiled her munificent smile. Fiamma obeyed, walking behind and pushing Miss G up the hill with her second finger on her back.

"Take off your things, girls; go on," Miss G said, as we gaped at the edge of the water, hesitating.

She unzipped her jumpsuit with one quick gesture, standing firm and lithe, her toes curling over the edge of the concrete. She was smooth and straight as a statue. Her bronzed skin was strange in the moonlight, the deeper dark of the shadow between her legs as quiet and mysterious as a shell.

"You're going to catch a fly," she told Fuzzie, who stood with her big mouth wide open.

"Do you think you're going to be run over by a bus and found without your knickers?" she asked Pamela, who was later to be so good at sex but now clutched her pajama bottoms, protectively.

Miss G lifted her arms, rose on her toes, and dived into the water. She splashed us and told us to get in. "What are you waiting for, kingdom come?" she asked. Then she turned and struck out strongly across the water, reaching valiantly with long arms, kicking up a silver spray in the moonlight.

Fiamma was the first to step out of her pajamas, unashamed. Naked in the moonlight, her white body shone softly. She was slimmer than most of us and lighter-boned. She carried her head high, tilted slightly to one side as though it might roll off. Because we were reading *The Tempest* that year, Miss Lacey called her Ariel.

We watched her open her arms to the stars and the night, and enter the water, her glittering body all gathered together like a white, lacquered bud.

For a moment we stood in silence and watched her swim. She was more at ease in water than on land. She was not good at any of the land sports we played: hockey and netball and rounders, but we had often found her in the pool at dawn, as though she had been there all night, beating back and forth, sending up a rainbow spray into the air, while the sun striped the sky pink and orange and red.

Di muttered, "She swims bloody fast," and threw off her dressing gown and pajamas. We all followed, throwing off our slippers into the wilting hydrangea bushes. We could see Pamela's ribs. Even Fuzzie threw off her vest and stood clutching her plump little boosies, trembling with embarrassment.

We plunged in a pack behind Fiamma, diving into a dream. Di swam breaststroke, her long, strong arms and legs stretched, lithe and fast; Meg swam sidestroke swiftly beside Di, her beautiful head, long neck, and big breasts dipping and rising over the water. Mary plowed through the pool, splashing, doing fast butterfly, and Ann, quick and neat and efficient, swam backstroke, with little splash, while Fuzzie, keeping her face in the water, not taking a breath for long stretches, her body wriggling like a worm, somehow kept up with the rest of us, swimming a crazy crawl. Sheila, too, who always tried hard, swam as fast as she could to keep up. Fiamma, who swam crawl so much faster than anyone else, swam out ahead of us, alone.

In the dim light and the warm water, we slipped back to a timeless time: we were small again, swimming through water to catch Miss G's phosphorescent, shining body. Soon we were swimming around her, under her, Fuzzie at her feet, Di at her head, Meg at her waist. Like minnows around the mother fish, we circled her, we brushed against her smooth body; we touched an arm, a leg, a toe; we felt her all over us in the water. She was swimming fast, turning her head back and forth, breathing in and out, beating the water evenly, surging beside us, and then she was lying still on her back, arms outstretched, staring up at the swirl of stars in the deep blue sky. We too lay on our backs and stared up at the stars. We thought we could hear the music of the spheres; the stars were singing to us; our mothers were chanting to us, we could hear the beating of Miss G's heart. Our heads spun. We floated on beside Miss G in the moonlight and the mysterious quiet of the night, the lights of the school glimmering faintly in the distance, only the crickets chirping.

We saw our mothers waving to us from afar; we saw them coming toward us in the starlight, their silver skirts blown against their bodies; we heard them calling our names with surprised delight. We watched them bending over and reaching out their arms and catching us up and swinging us through the air. We were flying. We were light as light can be. We left our bodies behind and flew, free through the air. We could smell the chlorine and the jasmine and the mysterious verbena scent of Miss G's skin. We felt the water ripple against our naked bodies like air, and we watched our mother's heads come down over us in the half dark to kiss our foreheads, our cheeks, our noses, our chins, and our lips, and their voices whispered, *Good night, good night.* The slapping and the splashing of the water kissed our faces, and the beating of our hearts said, *Good night, good night.*

Miss G was calling us softly. She made us get out of the water and stand by the edge of the pool in the pale white light. Water dripped from our hair. The moonshine was as warm as sun on our faces and on our new breasts. We stared at Miss G's strong, brown legs, the shadow of the shaved hair at the tops. She told us we were her girls. Otherwise she felt far away, removed. She paused. A blankness had come over her face. She said, "I feel at such a distance from the rest of the world."

What Miss G said about Fiamma

"COME UP HERE and sit by me," Miss G said, when Fiamma attempted to slip in late unnoticed and sit at the back of Miss G's room. Her face had a bright, soft look, and when she said Fiamma's name, her voice lingered. Fiamma moved slowly forward. "Burls, make room for her," Miss G told Fuzzie, who had to get up and move elsewhere.

We all sat quietly, waiting for Fiamma to take the only comfortable chair and settle herself down. Meg sat very upright on the floor, her shoulders pressed back and her head held high. Di lounged on Miss G's bed. Sheila sat on a hard stone step and squinted miserably. Mary sprawled on a stool with her legs open.

"Sit where I can see you. Perhaps you can save us, Fiamma," Miss G said.

"I am just a swimmer," Fiamma said.

"No, no false modesty here," Miss G said. She said Fiamma had great style; she had speed and endurance; only she could stay the course (Miss G was fond of nautical metaphors); only Fiamma had attained a consistent level of excellence. *She* was dedicated to the sport of swimming, despite her breathing problems, her homesickness, her father's illness. "You do not catch Fiamma lolling about in bed in the morning. She is up there, rising with the sun, in the water at first light, doing her fifty lengths," Miss G said, looking critically at Meg, who was sitting in her faded pink pajamas, stretching her neck, head to one side, pursing her lips, trying to look like Brigitte Bardot.

Meg slept heavily and late at school, with her dark hair hiding her flushed face, her body sprawled beneath her thin sheet, because she had to rise early at home in Barberton in the Eastern Transvaal. She was obliged to help with the family chores in the humid heat on holidays. She had to make the morning tea for her mother and father, help dress her little sisters, hang all the washing to dry, heap the furniture into the middle of the lounge and polish the floors.

"Unlike Burls, who never gets her racing turns right, Fiamma can turn in a flash. Why can she turn so fast, while Burls takes her sweet time and creates such a lot of unncessary splash? Watch how Fiamma does it," Miss G advised Fuzzie, who sat pressing her fat knees to the floor. "Of course, if you were to lose a few pounds, now, that would also help, you would not have so much mass to move." Fuzzie blinked her close-set, green eyes.

Only Fiamma could make a straight enough dive, Miss G pointed out to Mary, who was clumsy but quick, who had trouble keeping her long body in a straight line and her feet together when she entered the water.

"As for Lindt, she's not willing to take a risk: too cautious, too crafty, too busy weighing the odds."

Miss G said only Fiamma could open her arms wide enough to the sky when she swallow-dived. Only Fiamma was willing to give her all, to throw herself into the air with reckless abandon. What was the matter with the Trevelyan twins? she wanted to know. Why did they not have the necessary spring, the surge, the courage? What was wrong with Lizzie? What made her so precious? Why was she trying to be so perfect? What was wrong with all the rest of us? Why were we so ordinary, so dull, so reluctant to take a chance, to do something reckless and wild? Why did we leave Fiamma to blaze our trail?

Following Fiamma

Miss G followed Fiamma,
Watched her with dark eyes
Hurrying down the corridor,
Brightening when Fiamma she spied.

THE GRASS WAS DRY and dusty now. The seringa tree drooped over the wooden love seat in the corner. The pale wisteria petals fell to the ground. We watched Miss G walk behind Fiamma as she sauntered down the stone steps and along the edge of the prefects' square lawn. When Fiamma paused to look at a dry leaf stirring, a dove's wings beating, a swirl of dust, Miss G paused, too, and stared at a boot or flecked an imaginary spot of lint from her jumpsuit. When Fiamma turned around, feeling Miss G behind her, Miss G hurried by.

It was clear to us, she was no longer satisfied to see Fiamma in her room in the evenings or in the afternoons at the pool, gazing at Fiamma as she did a back flip from the high board, her luminous eyes straining in the sun. It was not enough for her to turn her head back and forth, as though she were watching a tennis match, as Fiamma skimmed up and down the water, the spray splashing Miss G's face, or to run up and down the edge of the pool through swimming heats, shouting her name like a rallying cry. It was not enough for her to feed Fiamma glucose with a spoon out of the blue-and-white tin between races or massage her feet, so that she did not get cramps, or rub her back with a towel. It was not even enough to call her by her Christian name.

If Fiamma were unable to sleep in the hot, dry nights, if she had one of her frequent attacks, her shallow cough keeping us awake, her breath coming in short, sharp pants, it was not into Mrs. Looney's room that she went for comfort. Night after night Miss G would come to see if Fiamma were well. She would tell Fiamma to follow her to her room. She would allow her to sit in her white smocked nightdress in her wide wicker chair and sip hot cocoa or wine. She slipped Fiamma past Mrs. Looney's room quietly and brought her back into the dormitory and sat on her bed and waited while she knelt and said her prayers in Italian and asked God to make her father well. Miss G tucked the sheet around her gently and arranged her mosquito netting over her bed carefully, so that she would not be bitten.

She made Fiamma promise that if anything were wrong she would come to her, but she never did. We would hear her ragged breathing and the pumping of the inhaler in the night. We could hear her tossing and turning. Miss G came so often that Fuzzie giggled, and Pamela jumped out of her bed and twitched her thin hips suggestively in the shadows, and all the rest whispered.

And now she had taken to following Fiamma about in the day as well. Ann watched her follow Fiamma along the pergola and said, "She's cracking up." We all watched her striding out, slightly flat-footed in her boots, blinking her dark eyes in the glare of light, hunting for Fiamma in the vast garden.

It was easy to lose a girl out there, and Fiamma always managed to disappear. We did not know where she went, or how she did it. Despite the rules, she was always going off on her own. We considered that she made no effort to fit in, to join our group. Before we could snub her, she snubbed us. Even worse, she seemed simply to ignore us. She was thinking of other things. She did not even notice our slights or understand our sarcasm. She smiled at us as she slipped by, dreaming, perhaps, of the cannas flaming orange and red at the edge of the terraced lawns of her villa by the lake.

It was not that she was unkind to us. She never raised her voice, or said anything hurtful. On the contrary, she was given to sudden and unexpected acts of kindness. When Bobby Joe had the chicken pox, Fiamma rose early and picked flowers and thrust them, still wet with dew, through the window at the san. She gave up the role of sleeping beauty to Meg in the school pageant even though the whole class had voted to give it to Fiamma. "You will do it much better than I will," she told Meg, who afterward bore a grudge against her.

Fiamma spoke of honor and loyalty and fidelity, but we considered she was playacting, and thought her kindness was condescension and her talk of higher things showing off and silliness. "Her Royal Highness is holding forth again," Di would say.

We thought her clothes pretentious and strange. In the evenings when we were allowed to change out of our uniforms, she wore dresses with labels from the big London shops: Liberty's or Harrods, dresses that looked babyish and odd with flowers embroidered in the smocking on her budding bosoms. She wore shoes with bars across the insteps and buttoned with a buttonhook. She threaded silk ribbons through her thick plait. She liked to dress up and act, and she loved the films they showed us once a month in the assembly room through a flickering projector, which was always breaking down.

Fuzzie sometimes said, "Perhaps she is not used to girls, to young people; she is accustomed to being shut up in an old house with her peculiar father and some old servant. Perhaps she would like to be our friend." But no one paid attention to Fuzzie.

We watched Miss G stride through the garden anxiously, hunting for Fiamma in all the cool, shady places where she sometimes hid from us: behind the hydrangeas, or in the dark, heavy branches of the loquat tree, which hung down so low they touched the smooth, dark earth.

We followed Miss G as she followed Fiamma. She went so far as to walk across the veld to the river and the graves in search of her. We were not allowed to swim the river because of the bilharzia, which infected many of the waters of that region, and the area around the graves was out-of-bounds, but as the heat increased in the summer months and the drought continued, and as the pool was not always available to the girls on the swimming team, we took to tucking up our tunics in our pants and running across the veld to linger in the shade of the wattles and the willows along the riverbanks. We would wade in the river, the brown, half-stagnant water rising up to our thighs.

None of the elderly spinster teachers remonstrated. None of them came to look for us. None of them cared. They did not care about much, during those dog days. They dragged themselves into the classrooms in a state of disarray in the mornings, sitting on dusty platforms, their legs carelessly apart, with the girls giggling and peeping up their skirts. Even Miss Lacey sat mopping her pale brow, stunned by the heat, the dry air, the continuous drought, letting us read popular novels in class. A general lethargy had crept over the staff.

Ann said there was more wine drinking than there should have been in the staff room at night. She had heard raucous laughter. She had seen bottles. She had glimpsed Mrs. Keilly, the geography teacher, staggering down the corridor as though she had no idea where she was. Miss Nieven herself seemed permanently unavailable, shut up in the fastness of her cool study. It was said that she was ill, though no one was able to confirm this report. We were left to our own devices much of the afternoon.

When Miss G caught sight of us following her, she asked what we were doing, but before we could answer, she said, "Has anyone seen Fiamma?" putting her hand up to shield her eyes from the blinding glare. "Have you not seen her anywhere?"

"No," Meg said, she had not. Could we not help in some way, perhaps, Meg asked, but we lowered our gaze, looked away so as not to see the expression of despair in Miss G's eyes. We were ashamed of her shame.

The air near the river was heavy and redolent with the odors from the latrines and the thick smell of stagnant water. The water was evaporating fast, leaving the banks slimy and slippery, the drying mud gray and cracked. The sun burned down through the slate gray haze. Several girls from the matriculation class, who should have been studying, sat by the water, half naked, their bare feet dangling, their fair arms and legs and unprotected faces burning, their skin peeling in wide strips from their shoulders, exposing livid patches of purple. Sheila walked in the riverbed with her tunic tucked up in her pants, the mud seeping up her calves, pretending to be a pirate.

"Over there," Bobby Joe said suddenly, "there she is!" and pointed to where Fiamma lay in the river. She was lying naked in the dark water, her light hair loose, letting the sluggish current catch her up and carry her slowly along for a way, reaching out lazily to grasp at overhanging willow branches.

We heard Miss G cry half in warning, half in salute. "Oh! Fiamma!"

How Miss G made Fiamma talk of her home

IT WAS LATE, and we were weary and hot, worn out with swimming, wine, Miss G's words, and the increasing heat. We had been sitting cramped and uncomfortable on the floor in her room for hours, or, if we were lucky, perched on her bed.

Only Fiamma sat in the comfortable chair, staring absently before her. She had come in after everyone else and nodded off in her chair by the window. Only she was allowed to come in late; to swing slowly out of the swimming pool in the middle of swimming practice and stand, dreaming, in the sun, staring into the middle distance while the water ran off her white body in silver strands; to lie by the side of the pool during practice in the shade of the mimosa tree with her towel over her shoulders.

"How much land did you say your father owns?" Miss G asked her once again, leaning toward her in her wicker chair. Miss G was fascinated by the aristocracy. We often saw her reading women's magazines with pictures of the Royal Family on the cover, holding the magazine under the desk when she had to supervise our homework. She claimed to have been presented to Prince Philip at court when she had won her medal. She told us that he was from a much better family than that of the Queen, whose ancestors could hardly speak English, coming as they did from a minor German family and having to change their name so that it sounded English.

It was Miss G who told us about Fiamma's pedigree, the history of her family, her place in society. She loved more than anything to make Fiamma describe her house by the lake.

We sat before her and rolled our eyes and flared our eyebrows at one another, blew out our cheeks, sighed, and shifted about, but Fiamma went on and on in her singsong voice. Perhaps she was carried away by her own words, her memories of home, of happier days with her father, who was increasingly ill with bouts of high fever and delirium. While she spoke, Miss G moved her lips as though she were the one speaking.

Fiamma said her house was surrounded by beautiful, regular gardens with gravel paths and ancient trees and a stone wall. It was old and very large. One day it would all be hers, although she knew her mother would try to lay claim to it for her half sister's sake.

There was a profusion of cut flowers in every room — roses and sweet peas and lilacs, lilies and peonies and baby's breath. In the entrance hall there was a forest of flowers. It was like a hothouse, and there was the sweet smell of the many flowers mingled with some other smell, like that of incense. It made Fiamma think of funerals and weddings at the same time.

There were many old, dark paintings in niches, lit up with little lamps hung over the gold-embossed frames. Many were old still lifes where the half-peeled fruit or bleeding hare was barely visible. In one of the paintings two French sisters stare out of the canvas with a pleased expression, as though they are proud of what they are doing. Their hair is coiffed high on their heads, and their stiff breasts are completely bare. One of the women holds the nipple of the other delicately between her curved white finger and thumb.

Her father also owned a famous collection of diamonds, Fiamma said. There was a famous yellow one and a famous blue one, which was supposed to bring bad luck. This was why they had come to our country: her father was buying diamonds for his collection. He had visited Kimberley before going on to the game reserve where he had fallen ill.

When she stopped speaking, Miss G made her go on. "How many servants did you say there were, tending the garden?" she asked while we covered our yawns with our hands and shifted our weight uncomfortably on Miss G's carpet or on the hard floor. Fiamma had never counted all the servants. She said she and her father ate dinner on the stone terrace, often alone. In the candlelight, her father looked so handsome in his cream linen trousers, his damp, dark hair brushed back smoothly. He asked her about her life and listened to her with great interest, as though she were a grown-up. He had read everything, she maintained, all the books we read at school. They talked about Rider Haggard and Kipling and Dickens. He knew all about Miss Havisham walking around and around the decaying bridal feast and about Uriah Heep's damp hands. He, too, loved to watch her swim. When she was a small girl, he had taken her to see walled medieval towns, poppies growing through the stone, the sun setting over the sea at Naples. There she had broken a glass and cut her feet.

Fortunately, Miss G was not as interested in Fiamma's father as she was in her house, her paintings, and her habits, and we were allowed to go to bed.

We left Fiamma behind in Miss G's room, imagining her standing and staring out the window while Miss G paced up and down restlessly, in her khaki overalls, or worse.

Miss G made us suffer

"IS FIAMMA HERE?" Miss G said, as we shuffled into her hot room in our pajamas and slippers, half asleep. It was late, but Miss G could not sleep, and so she had called us into her room to enlighten us. The windows were closed on the hot night, but we could hear the dry wind beating in the palms.

"Where is Fiamma? Why has she not come? I told you to bring all the girls on the team, Radfield," Miss G said, looking anxiously around her room for Fiamma.

Di did not answer. Fiamma had mumbled something rude to her in Italian and refused to rise. "You'll get me into trouble," she had said, but Fiamma went back to sleep.

"She must be unwell, poor girl. Is she unwell? Now she swam well today," Miss G said, looking at Fuzzie. "Why can't you swim as well as she does, Burls?"

She told us to find a perch, picked up her glass of mixed red and white wine, and wiped her wide lips. We could see she was working herself up. She was trying to distract herself from her agony. For a moment we thought she might find someone else to distract her, but her gaze fell again on Fuzzie.

Her father, everyone knew, had contributed hundreds of pounds to the swimming team fund so that Miss G would put her on the team. Everyone knew, too, that she had been expelled from her former school, though no one knew why.

"Burls-the-Bear, excuse my French, but you swam like shit

again today," Miss G said, and we could not help laughing. We loved it when she swore and said, "Excuse my French." Fuzzie blushed as bright pink as her pajamas; and her double chins pressed down upon her chest. She sat cross-legged, her fat knees pressing against the floor.

"What's the matter with you, Burls? Thinking about the boys again?"

Fuzzie did not reply but only blushed redder, so that her freckles disappeared, and her head sank further onto her chest. Everyone was staring at her, laughing, except for Meg, who looked as though she were about to weep. Fuzzie was watching her hand trace the sinister, blue flower pattern of Miss G's carpet.

"What, no reply from Burls? Perhaps it's about the girls that she's thinking?"

We laughed even louder at that, and Pamela made little kissing noises, and we put our arms around ourselves and rubbed our backs.

"No, I'm not thinking about either one," Fuzzie said, blinking her close-set eyes. We were all watching with secret delight, glad someone else was the target of Miss G's ire, as Fuzzie sank miserably into the blue flower pattern, her face flushed with shame.

"Why are you left wallowing around in the water when Fiamma passes you by? She must be exhausted after the way she swam today. Did she remain in the dormitory, or has she gone off somewhere on her own again? She's not ill, is she?" Miss G's voice rose to a panic pitch. She got up and walked back and forth across her room, her boots creaking. She scratched at the bristles at the back of her neck.

No one said anything.

"Don't any of you know? Don't you care? Lindt, what about you? You're supposed to be her friend, aren't you?"

"Yes, I am," Ann said, looking as though she were thinking about mathematics. "But I make it a rule not to talk about anyone behind her back."

"Very wise, Lindt, very wise," Miss G said, sitting down again and turning back to Fuzzie. She scratched her leg, saying, "Burls-the-Bear, now why isn't it Fuzzie-the-Fish? It could be Fuzzie-the-Fish, couldn't it? Actually, you do look a bit green, postively green around the gills tonight. Been eating chocolates on the sly, hey? You ought to watch your weight, don't you think?"

Fuzzie blinked, lowered her head, and said, "Yes, Miss G." No one laughed now.

She went on scratching. "I am only saying this for your own good, you know. No one else will tell you girls the truth. Your parents are too far away, and only I care about you. Obviously no one else does. I could tell you lies as everyone else does. I could tell Burls that she swam well, but what good would that do her? You have got to look into your heart and find the truth, and the truth is you are putting on weight. You look bloated, puffy. Can't you see it when you look in the miror? Are you blind, after all? If you cannot see it, there must be something wrong with you. You will never be able to swim well, if you put on any more weight. Did you ever see a fat swimmer? Besides, doesn't all that fat disgust you? Look at your arms, even they are getting fat. Now no more chocolates, hey? Promise me, will you?"

"Yes, I promise," Fuzzie muttered to the carpet.

"You'd better, if you want the boys to love you, and if you want to swim as well as Fiamma. Don't you want the boys to love you? Why do you eat so much? You ought to think about that; there must be a reason. You've got to find it out. Can't you tell me?"

"I don't know why, Miss G," Fuzzie said with a great sob. The tears were pouring down her fat cheeks, and Meg was weeping, too, in sympathy.

Miss G lit a cigarette and exhaled fast, scratching at her leg.

"What's the matter with you, Burls? Get up and go and find your friend," she concluded. "Go and see if she's all right, Burls, do you hear?" Fuzzie staggered out of the room, saying she had pins and needles in her peg legs.

The team's losses

MISS G WAS increasingly distracted as the long summer term wore on. She did not listen when we talked but gazed across the gray grass and the flowers strangled in the soil. She did not respond to us. She no longer talked about the truth or the wonderful things we could accomplish.

When she did speak, she fell silent suddenly and gazed toward the pool in the fading evening light. She had lost the direction of her thought. We waited for her to continue, but she scratched the back of her head and said, "What's the point? Go on, go and swim, girls, go along."

As we swam slowly up and down the pool, or even lay on our backs and stared at the red sky, she stood beside the pool in her swimming costume, her whistle hanging silently between her dry, chapped lips. She did not run up and down beside the pool as she used to do when we swam in the evening; she did not call our names. Sometimes she even forgot our names, calling Lindt, Radfield, and Kohler, Donovan. She never again called us to swim with her at midnight, despite the increasing December heat.

We all stared up at her in the long shadows of the evening light. We hardly recognized her. She had lost weight; deep, dark circles formed under her eyes; her breath smelled sour. She looked older, though we noticed she made an attempt to cover it up. She had taken to wearing makeup. She applied mascara to her eyelashes but would forget it was there and rub her eyes, causing it to run down her cheeks. She even colored her wide lips with a ghastly, dark rouge that gave her a hard air. She had dry patches on her skin and sores around her mouth. She scratched constantly. Her old skin ailment was acting up in the dry heat. We were afraid she would fall ill, or, worse, leave us. Sometimes she even even spoke of giving up teaching. "For the amount of money they pay us to do this, it isn't worth it," she said; no one appreciated her efforts. No one was grateful. No one cared. What was the point?

We no longer won any prizes. Di no longer flashed her shiny, pink gums and her strong, white teeth in the sun, her arms full of trophies. Instead, her arms hung limply by her sides, her empty hands clutching at the air. Our team came last or next to last. Kingsmead beat us. St. Andrews beat us. Even the convent schools beat us. We slunk back to the bus in the shadows, ashamed. We sat silently and gazed out the windows. We sang no triumphant songs. We scowled at Fiamma, who sat in silence beside Ann on the bus or walked past us with her head tilted and her distant air.

Staring up at Miss G as she stood vacantly by the side of the pool in the evening light, we could not believe that she had fallen for a girl who made no attempt to be charming, who had no desire to charm her, or anyone, who slipped by us like the moon through cloud. To us Fiamma seemed entirely unfeeling. We found her cold, through and through. She never seemed angry or sad or even amused. When we told one another jokes and laughed raucously, rolling about, holding our stomachs on the floor, she only fidgeted and left the room.

None of us could understand how Miss G could get excited

about a girl like her. Italians were supposed to be so passionate and temperamental. They were supposed to fall into rages, to express themselves in song. "Besides," Mary whispered, "Italians aren't blond."

When we complimented her, she shrugged her shoulders, indifferent, as though all she wanted was to pass unnoticed. She never took pains to impress, and yet we found her domineering and mysteriously willful. Ann helped her with her Afrikaans homework; Mary, with her science; Meg baked an extra batch of scones for her at domestic science, because she was not eating much; Sheila lent her silver pens, and she lost them in the grass. Her carelessness created havoc in our hearts.

When we spoke of love or attraction, she said nothing. She was always scrupulously polite, but she was always trying to escape us, slipping by coolly and boldly, as though she wished to make herself invisible.

We could not believe that Miss G, who had told us once she felt at a distance, felt far, far out at sea and alone, could be brought back in and made a fool of by this pale, careless girl.

What to do about Fiamma?

Meg wanted to be Brigitte Bardot,
Sheila, to be Scarlett.
All Ann wanted was to read Diderot,
But we all wanted to be Miss G's pet.

THE DOVES COOED in the eucalyptus trees. The wind stirred the dust across the dry veld, which had been set ablaze by one carelessly discarded cigarette stub, causing untold damage, reducing a thousand acres to a black stub-

ble. The thatched roofs of the round changing huts had caught
fire, saved only when the night watchman, John Mazaboko, had
come running with his hose.

The earth had cracked, and the roots of the flowers were
strangled in the soil. Only the red-hot pokers and the aloes with
their prickly pears still stood stiffly upright. The fan-shaped
sprinklers no longer waved back and forth in the evenings on
the lawns, cooling the air. When we went for walks in the afternoons, the dust was on our shoes and in our mouths. We were
not allowed to bathe at all now except in the basins that ran
along the center of the dormitories like a string of coffins. We
all splashed 4711 behind our ears and poured it between our
new bosoms. Di had put it in the wrong place and screamed
when it stung.

We were supposed to lie on our beds for two hours after
lunch because of the polio scare. There had been an outbreak
of it. The only newspaper available to us was the *Manchester
Guardian*, which gave us no local news anyway, but the teachers
told us terrible stories of children paralyzed from the waist
down, their limbs withered, pushed around in wheelchairs for
the rest of their lives.

Because of fear of contagion we were not allowed to go to the
few public places usually allowed us: the outing to the Pablo
Casals concert, the tour of the art museum. Even our Friday
visits to town for doctors' and dentists' appointments were can-
celed. We no longer went to lie under the sunlamp, burning off
our pimples. We no longer left the grounds at all. The iron gate
was kept closed except for the one Sunday a month when the
girls who had families in the area went home, and the rest of us
tried despererately to ingratiate ourselves with someone who
would take us along. Some of the parents, like Sandra's, had
sent for their children. Those who remained were to wear little

cotton bags with camphor around their necks. The teachers, too, lay on their beds for two hours after lunch.

We stood before the mirrors behind the basins in the long, narrow dormitory with its iron cots and whispered about Fiamma and Miss G. Meg pursed her heavy lips like Brigitte Bardot and lisped, "If Fiamma were kinder to Miss G, she would be kinder to us. Why doesn't she care for her?"

Bobby Joe glanced along the dormitory to Fiamma's bed at the end by the wall, where she lay, apparently sleeping, on her side, one arm above her head, and said, "She doesn't care for anyone." She seemed capable of sleeping for long hours, hardly moving on her bed.

Ann, on the bed next to Fiamma, said in her low, nasal voice, "It won't last; nothing lasts long with Miss G," and glowered in the background, looking glum, propped up on pillows, reading about revolutions. She read about the American Revolution, the Russian Revolution, the French Revolution. She read about the eighteen-century French philosophers in her history book: Rousseau and Diderot and Montesquieu, and about the Rights of Man.

Di said, "Perhaps, but in the meantime, I am getting impatient."

Di was half naked before the mirrors, using her school tie as a veil, dancing the Dance of the Seven Veils, pretending to be Salome, getting Herod to give her John the Baptist's head. Mary was dissecting a tadpole she had fished out of the pond to study for science.

Sheila lay on the bed beside Pamela, their feet in the air, comparing their beauty. Sheila was finding her own superior. She said there was nothing we could do about the situation anyway and added that she was trying to decide whether to be bold and rapacious like Scarlett O'Hara or good and meek like Melanie, but was leaning toward Scarlett. Di said she much preferred to be Becky Sharp than Amelia.

Fuzzie, who was singing *"La donna è mobile,"* trying to be Mimi Coertse, said she wanted to be Jane Eyre as a fierce wild child shut up in the red room, not as a meek and mild grown-up who wore gray and fell in love with Mr. Rochester.

Ann blew her thin nose and scolded us. She told us we were all vain, strutting about before the mirrors, and should stop thinking about ourselves and think instead of our fellow man, not trifle our lives away. Instead of hovering before the mirror, contemplating our images, we should be thinking about helping others. What about the poor, the hungry, the homeless, the natives?

When she rose and came over to us, approaching the mirror, she turned away from her reflection, her high, shiny forehead bulging like an egg, her little pig eyes glowing, and went on scolding us. We should all be thinking about the injustice of the natives' position in our country. Wasn't it time someone did something about that?

Mary said she had helped with the African Feeding Scheme in her holidays. She had fed starving little black children peanut-butter sandwiches.

But we went on dreaming of Miss G or Heathcliff, putting our hands between our legs. When Miss Lacey had asked how many girls would like to marry him, all the hands shot up.

Our favorite film stars were Ava Gardner and Gregory Peck. She was so beautiful and familiar, shining with her own light, and he, though dark and handsome and smooth, was all mysteriously wrapped up in a suit. Which one to choose? We wanted them both. Only Miss G was both familiar and mysterious, beautiful and dark at the same time; only she was capable of arousing all our desires.

But why did she desire Fiamma?

Pamela said she thought Fiamma was keeping some deep, dark secret from us. "Perhaps she had a lover in Italy?" she suggested and turned her foot to a more advantageous position in the light. "Can't you see mine is much prettier than yours?" she told Sheila.

"Perhaps she had lots!" Fuzzie exclaimed loudly, but Fiamma did not stir.

"Do you think she is really asleep?" Lizzie asked Ann, who went back to her bed and peered down at Fiamma, who, as though she felt our gaze on her, or had been listening all along, stirred, rose languidly from her bed, went over to the basins, and began scrubbing her cheeks with soap and a toothbrush. She always did that to preserve her creamy complexion.

We pretended to read but spied on her. Di went back to being Salome and Fuzzie, to singing *"La donna è mobile."* Mary said she was going to flush the tadpole down the toilet.

We were always spying on her. Sheila, who enjoyed it, looked on, as Fiamma scrubbed absentmindedly. She whispered, "Her Royal must be preparing for Miss G."

"Now Her Royal must be thirsty," Meg observed, when Fiamma added an Alka-Seltzer capsule to a glass of water to make it fizz, because she never drank flat water. Meg was never given even the pocket money to buy her sanitary towels and was obliged to borrow them from Di.

Di whispered that Fiamma washed her hair with fresh lemon to heighten its blond lights, and took baths in milk to make her skin white. Fuzzie said it was champagne.

The twins rose from their beds. One put her panama hat on her head and walked over to the door. She pretended to come in the door, imitating the way Fiamma curtsied when she shook hands with adults, making a brief bob. They bobbed at one another, giggling. One said, "Your Royal Highness, how delightful, how lovely of you to come to tea."

There was a shuffling at the door, and everyone ran back to her bed. We watched the door open. Miss G came in, wearing her usual khaki jumpsuit and boots.

"What's all this? You are supposed to be resting. What's going on?" she asked, as though there had been an outbreak of fire.

No one answered. "Fiamma, are you feeling all right, dear? No bad news about your father, was there?" she asked anxiously, striding over to her. Fiamma shrugged sulkily and said she was fine and went on scrubbing her cheeks.

"Better come with me, darling," she said in a hoarse voice.

"I'm fine, at the moment," Fiamma said fiercely, glaring at Miss G and at us as well. We were having a fit of suppressed giggles and making little kissing faces behind our books.

Miss G said, "Just come with me."

Fiamma sighed, rinsing off her brush and taking her sweet time. She made Miss G wait. She put on her socks and shoes. Then she gathered up her book. Miss G followed each movement with her ardent gaze.

So did we. She crossed the dormitory in silence like a queen, accepting Miss G's silent tribute, her head tilted very slightly to one side. There was something awesome about her. She was irresistible; she always got her way. We thought she had put a spell on Miss G.

We tiptoed in our socks down the corridor to Miss G's half-open door. We hovered there, listening and trying to see what was happening inside, pushing one another out of the way. We caught a glimpse of Fiamma, as she sat in state in Miss G's wide wicker chair. Her head was poised delicately on her long neck, her languid locks on her collarbone. She stared ahead, reading the bound book that lay in her lap and sulkily sipping from a big cup of cocoa, as Miss G sat at her feet. What was she sulking about? we wanted to know.

Miss G got as close as she could, smiling up at her. She had her big hands around her knees. She was glowing, burning; she was on fire.

We watched, our hearts pounding, waiting for something to happen. But it did not: nothing happened! Fiamma went on reading. She rose and stood silently by the window, gazing at the sky, with her head tilted a little, pulling idly at a loose lock of hair. We had no idea what she was thinking about. All we knew was that Miss G adored her.

What did Miss G see in Fiamma?

WE LAY whispering in the hot, dark dormitory on our hard, narrow beds, troubled by mosquitoes and dreams. Fiamma was with Miss G, once again. As usual, Ann perched with her torch in the window seat, reading her book. She said it was Fiamma's illness and loneliness, her distance from the rest of us, that drew Miss G irresistibly to her. "She identifies with Fiamma's incapacity to fit in," Ann said, twisting her mouth sightly to one side.

It was true that Fiamma took part less and less in our competitions and fierce jealousies. She seemed more interested in inanimate things, trees, rocks, even ants, than in us. We saw her sit for hours, watching the red ants crawl under a log. Was she dreaming of her past, or some unknown future? Did she perhaps see, in her mind's eye, some old Milanese church, where, pushing aside the heavy leather curtain and breathing in the odors of incense rising from the censers, watching the gold light coming in from a high window aslant, she slipped quietly into a pew beside some dark, unshaven man? Did she enjoy her solitude, gathering herself together and escaping from the din and strife around her? Or was she lonely? Did she find peace? Or did she long to join in our games?

She answered our questions about her life briefly but never asked about ours. She seemed to hear and see us all, but distantly, as through a pane of pebbled glass. We never felt she preferred one or the other of us, not even Ann, who was supposed to be her best friend.

Fuzzie said she did not know about Fiamma anymore. Everything was all confused in Fuzzie's mind, since they took her mother away, last year. She wasn't sure what she had made up, and what had really happened. When she came back from a singing lesson one day during the holidays, the house was empty. Her mother was no longer in her room, brushing her long, dark hair, nor was she out in the hothouse, growing her orchids, rather than the dahlias she preferred. They had taken her away to the asylum, and she had died in a fire, which spread because the young psychiatrist had forgotten to do the fire drill properly.

Fuzzie said she kept imagining her mother in her white dress, flitting up and down the corridor, rattling the doorknobs, screaming for help. Fuzzie's father always made a point of telling everyone that, although his wife was Jewish, he himself was Christian.

Ann said, "Fiamma has secrets like everyone else." Some of them Ann had learned. She knew most of our secrets. When Fiamma was visiting Ann's farm for the holidays, Fiamma had told her the story of how her mother had left her father after their wedding night. He had married beneath himself, for love. She may have been the housekeeper or a nurse, a pretty, strong-willed woman with fair, curly hair and a ruddy complexion. She already had a child in tow. His family was against the match, but he married her anyway. After their wedding night —

Fiamma never knew exactly what happened but suspected her mother had actually beaten him after he finished forcing himself on her — her mother went off to Milan. Apparently she was pregnant with Fiamma already, and nine months later came back to the villa to leave the baby by the lake.

The mother and half sister lived in Milan with another man, perhaps several men in succession. Fiamma visited them a couple of times in a small, dark flat near the Duomo, and some man was always lurking around behind the thick, green curtains that divided the rooms. All the furniture was highly polished, and there were artificial flowers in vases on the marble mantelpieces. Fiamma's father did not like her to go there. He was frightened of her mother. "He says she's unscrupulous and ambitious, that she's a whore," she told Ann.

Fiamma's mother adored Fiamma's half sister, who lay in a dark room with the curtains drawn. Fiamma had only seen her once. She wore her hair short with a curl matted down with grease on her forehead and spoke in an affected drawl. She smelled of onions, which her mother gave her for her health, and as a result everyone called her Cipolla, meaning "onion." She was supposed to be suffering from some illness. "She likes to pull the wings off flies," Fiamma told Ann.

Di said in her opinion Miss G was enamored of Fiamma because she was a rich princess. Di said Miss G was fascinated by status. But Di did not even believe that Fiamma was an aristocrat. She had never mentioned her title, after all.

Lizzie said it was Fiamma's elegance: the way she walked and the way she moved her hands so smoothly in the air.

Meg, who read romances, said it was a sort of rapture — that was the word that would describe it in a romance. Miss G was enraptured by the way Fiamma flung open a door or a window, stepped out into the light, and seemed immediately to own the place; her high-handedness and haughty stare. It was because she liked to be herself — careless, dauntless, elegant.

Everyone agreed Fiamma was beautiful, but there were other beautiful girls on our team, after all. There was Meg herself and Di, of course. Fiamma was an exceptional swimmer, but we had other good swimmers as well. Di could beat her at breaststroke, and Ann at backstroke, but no one could surpass her at crawl, and crawl, of course, is the fastest one of all.

Despite Miss G's opinion Bobby Joe was much braver than Fiamma. When Bobby Joe was allowed to exercise the horses that were kept for the paying pupils, she trick-rode. She could stand up on the horse and hang down below its belly. She could do a double back flip from the high board and Fiamma only a single, but none of us was more graceful than Fiamma.

Fiamma told Ann that she found Miss G overbearing, missing the point, which was not lost on the rest of us. "Do you know what she did?" Fiamma said. "She left a pair of swimming goggles on my dresser with a little note, wishing me a happy birthday. I don't know how she knew it was my birthday."

Di said, "Whatever the reason, Miss G's passion is not reciprocated. She does not impress Fiamma at all." At the same time, we knew perfectly well, Miss G was falling more and more desperately in love with her.

What Di Radfield did not tell the detective

D I DID NOT TELL the detective what had happened in the changing hut. She did not want to, when he questioned her after Fiamma disappeared. He was a young man, who must have just finished his training — it was probably his first case.

He seemed ill at ease in her presence, as if he were the one who had committed the crime. He sat there chewing gum, sweating heavily, talking about the drought, and smelling of B.O. Di tried to draw back from him, but she was trapped in the corner of the library. There was no air in there, because the windows and the shutters were closed on the heat.

She found something very grating about the stupid jokes he kept making. He even snickered a couple of times. He was an Afrikaner idjut, she told us afterwards.

At first he just sat there with a fat file filled with papers, then he asked her all the wrong questions. He asked her if she had a boyfriend, making her furious. She wanted to slam her fist down on the table, but she just asked him if he had ever heard of the expression "It's none of your business." He opened his file and read his notes and questioned her about her father's drinking and his suicide, and her sister finding him in the bath, his wrists slit, the blood turning the water pink. Miss Nieven must have given him all sorts of information, because he asked why, when Miss Nieven had said she could go home at that time, Di had preferred to go back to swimming practice.

Di could still see her father in the narrow hallway of their house with the "Cries of London" paintings on the walls. He was balding and his pate was shiny, and he had an orange in his hands. He was explaining, "If you cut it in half you have two parts; if you cut it again, you have four." That's all she remembered of his words.

Di did not say anything about what happened at the pool that morning early, either. She had just arrived to practice her racing starts and found Miss G striding up and down the edge of the pool in her black bathing costume. She could see the shimmer of sweat on her strong arms and the dark shadow of the shaved hair between her strong, brown legs. Miss G was watching Fiamma dive and swim fast, up and down the pool, doing crawl for one length, making a racing turn, and then doing backstroke for the next. She was showing off, doing back or swallow dives from the high board, fearlessly. There were only a few other girls swimming at that early hour.

The pool lay in the soft shadows of the mimosas and the wilting blue hydrangeas. The cool, clear water shone a yellow-green, and dew glittered like splintered glass on the gray grass.

Di tried to keep up with Fiamma, but she could not. She climbed out of the water and practiced her racing starts, smacking her stomach flat on the surface of the water each time. Then Fiamma got out of the pool and did a perfect swallow dive from the high board, opening her arms on the rising sun and orange sky. It was too much.

Di went into one of the small thatched-roofed changing huts. She had just removed her black racing costume and tossed it in a crumpled heap onto the polished floor, and was standing naked in a corner under the bare rafters, when she heard the hinges of the wooden door squeak and felt a rush of cooler air. She remained silent, hidden in the shadows, as Fiamma entered.

Di was not sure why she hid there, what she was planning to do, if anything. She watched Miss G follow Fiamma into the changing room with the light behind her. Di could not see Fiamma's face because she had turned her back. Slowly Fiamma slipped her arms out of her straps and folded down the top of her swimming suit. She spread her arms out on either side and shook her smooth shoulders in a sort of dance. Little drops of water fell onto the concrete floor from the tips of her fluttering fingers. She stepped out of her swimsuit. Di saw her naked back, bare white shoulders, and damp skin, clothed only in the cool morning air.

All the while, Di heard the bells chiming loudly, calling us to assembly, and then, as though awakened by the bells, the crowing of the cocks.

There was not a word spoken. Miss G was watching Fiamma, and her face was wet, her mouth slightly open. Then she moved toward Fiamma, slowly, and put her arms gently around her. She lowered her dark head to Fiamma's boosie and sucked, making noises like a baby. Di wanted to weep because Miss G had never even touched her boosies.

Then Fiamma pushed Miss G away from her, roughly. "Please," Miss G implored. Fiamma said, "Can't you just leave me *alone*," and walked past Miss G and out of the changing room, leaving the door ajar. Di saw the grass shining white in the early morning light, and the soft flowers on the mimosa trees, like snow on the thin branches. She put on her tunic quickly and picked up her panama hat and ran down the bank toward the school.

How we upset Fiamma

A NN WAS PERCHED on the window seat, reading about Winston Churchill and the armored train and the Boer War in the light of her yellow torch. Sheila was telling a story about violent death. All her plots ended violently. The Trevelyans were lying side-by-side in bed, whispering about our team's recent failures. "Even Helpmekaar High beat us," Bobby Joe said with disgust.

Ann looked up from her book and whispered, "Miss G's lost interest in our winning. She doesn't desire us to win anymore."

Di said, "She's all washed up."

Bobby Joe said, "She's gone completely barmy."

Fuzzie said, "She keeps picking on me. She keeps telling me I'm too fat. Does she think I want to be fat?"

Ann said, "She tells me I have a blight of blackheads on my nose, and my nails are dirty, and I should try and walk like Fiamma."

Meg whispered to Fiamma, who was lying on her back in the moonlight and staring up at the ceiling, "I wish Miss G liked me as much as she does you. What did you do to make her like you so much?" Fiamma rolled over without answering.

Pamela made little kissing noises in the dark, and got up and twitched her thin hips. We all laughed.

Bobby Joe said, "If I hear about Fiamma's villa one more time, I'll strangle her."

Fiamma rolled back and said, "What do you want me to do? She makes me describe it."

Bobby Jean said, "You could at least keep it short and sweet."

Meg said, "If you were sweeter to Miss G, do you see, she would be sweeter to us. She's unhappy, because you are not nice to her, because you either ignore her or are rude to her. That's why she picks on us."

Bobby Joe made kissing noises in the dark and rose from her bed and pulled Bobby Jean out. They danced the tango up and down the dormitory, leaning forward and back while Fuzzie sang: Ta-da-da-dada, ta-da-dada. We all laughed loudly. Mary told us to shut up, we would wake Mrs. Looney.

Fiamma sat up in the moonlight in her smocked nightdress. She looked around at us and said in her bored English voice, "I am not sure you know what you are suggesting."

Di said, "You shouldn't be so bloody superior all the time. You think you're better than everyone else, don't you — even better than Miss G. What right do you have to be so bloody stuck-up?"

Fiamma flopped down again on the bed and turned her narrow buttocks into the air and her face into the pillow.

Meg said, "You could be nicer to her for our sakes, don't you see, just to make our lives easier, even if you don't want to."

Mary said, "The means justifies the end, like she says."

Ann dusted the back of Fiamma's head with the beam of her yellow torch and said, "Lots of people in history have sacrificed themselves for others. God even asked Abraham to kill his own son, and he was going to do it. Judith sacrificed herself, and so did Cleopatra with the asp at her bosom, and so did Lucretia. We should all sacrifice ourselves for the common good, to relieve the suffering of others. I would be happy to sacrifice myself for others, if someone wanted me to do it."

PART THREE
THE DINNER

+>-<+

What we talk about

A STARCHED WHITE tablecloth, willow-pattern plates, cut glass, and shimmering cutlery array the trestle table that has been set up in the shade for our feast. White printed menus are propped up in silver holders. Frosted silver pitchers of iced water lie at either end. There are camphor candles in glass bowls all along the table to keep off the mosquitoes.

Meg, the only one wearing a low-cut dress, waves her hand smoothly in the air and lisps, "It looks like a wedding."

Fuzzie has never married, though she has been in love so many times: "Every four weeks, when the moon is full." Her freckled skin is still smooth, and she is no longer ungainly, but she still has the apprehension in her close-set green eyes that makes us, too, apprehensive, as it always did.

"Let's hope the food's improved. Do you remember that ghastly, lumpy porridge they made us eat every morning?" Meg says, pulling a sour face. Di reminds us what wonderful scones Meg made in domestic science. Ann, with that twist to her thin lips that makes her seem detached from what she says, reminds us that Meg, despite her romantic air, was a practical girl, a realist, who said she would marry a rich man. Meg looks from Di to Ann and laughs. "And I did." She still has her leafy scent.

Fuzzie says, "I'm starving." As she leans across the table to reach for the menu, she looks almost willowy. Fuzzie, so fat as a young girl, has become thin. Her hem hangs sadly to one side, and she has tied around her neck a cheap pink scarf, which clashes with her hair, cropped short now but still very red and curly.

Ann whispers to Sheila that she wonders if Fuzzie gave her fortune away to charity in a manic fit. "Do you suppose she still wears her vest as she did as a child, even in the worst heat?" Ann asks.

"Probably," says Sheila, who believes what has happened before will happen again.

"Sit by me, Meg," says Di, now heavy, sitting down at the head of the table. "You sit over there, Fuzzie."

Fuzzie has spent years sitting on the veranda staring at the morning glory creeping up the walls of the mental hospital. Now she sits in the middle of the long trestle table between the snub-nosed Trevelyans. Her years in the asylum, in spite of her repeated shock treatments, seem to have preserved her youthfulness. She looks like a fawn, gentle and timorous, as she bends over the bright anemones in the center of the table and sniffs, saying with surprise, "But they have no smell!"

Sheila sits at the other end of the long table beside Mary and Pamela, the girl who always got less than 10 percent in maths. Pamela is still as thin as ever but now has varicose veins in her legs from all the standing she has had to do while binding books. Sheila frowns. Perhaps she is thinking of her work. She wanted to be a writer like Alan Paton, and write a sentence like his about all the roads leading to Johannesburg, but she has only written thrillers, all of them about murdered girls.

Mary, who has become a doctor, looks jowly, but we recognize elements of the uncomplicated girl in her smile, bowl-cut hair, and shapeless dress.

We sit down, one after the other. Everyone sits apart. We gaze blankly at one another. Ann still has her perpetual cold. She looks slightly feverish, and her high forehead and protuberant eyes shine.

We are all bored. We have nothing to say to one another, after all this time. And if anyone wanted to speak, where on earth would she begin? What do we all expect?

Di jerks her head back and says to Meg, "Tell me what has happened to you."

Meg sits very stiffly, in silence, her shoulders pressed back, her head held high. She looks as though she has practiced this position before a mirror and found it advantageous. She shakes her head and says, "Nothing much, really. It's extraordinary. So many years, without anything special happening."

Ann, who sits opposite Meg, blows her nose and says in her nasal voice, "Oh, come on, Meg, something must have."

Meg says, "Well, I did marry a lovely, rich pediatrician. I actually fell in love with him when I saw him with children. It was the way he put his hand on their heads, ever so gently."

Di looks at Meg and says sadly, "Ah, Meg in love."

Meg goes on, with her slight lisp, "But we have not had children, ourselves. We tried everything, even hormones from menopausal Italian nuns. But we do have one another. We are very happy. We travel. We have a lovely house; I grow roses, you know. You see, nothing out of the ordinary."

Di says, "Really so happy? It seems to me I am left with only objects. Two of my husbands have gone, my children are scattered, and my dog has died." She looks around the veranda, as though the missing might be here in the shadows.

The veranda has grown shabby; the damp has peeled the

paint; there is dust in the corners — even the proteas in the brass bowl look dusty; spiderwebs hang from the beams. We sip drinks in the late afternoon shadows. There is the smell of damp earth. Lizzie rises suddenly, scraping back the long bench on the polished floor and making off with an air of secrecy. She is still slim and elegant, and her gray hair hangs straight to her shoulders. We watch her walking out into the garden, alone.

We break the silence again by speaking about the condition of the country. Ann, who was always interested in it and always went into things in depth, has written several books on the troubles of our country, which were translated widely, even into Japanese. She removes something from a tooth with her nail and says the place is less changed than it should be.

"To tell you the truth, I am sick and tired of talking about this country, sick of it!" Di says.

The silence drops again. We watch the breeze lifting the branches and the lawns running down and down, falling away, strange and gray in the twilight like the mountains of the moon. We listen to the chiming of the clock. Something silver glimmers in the distance and is gone.

Meg reminds us how Di wanted to be a dancer like Margot Fonteyn and kept hoping she would stop growing, but she didn't. She looks as tall and as broad-shouldered as a man.

Di drinks hard liquor fast, swinging her crossed leg. She has married three times: number one, one of her teachers at the Royal Ballet, left her for a black professor of mathematics; number two, a very rich American, died and left her a fortune. Now she has her vast house, acres and acres of empty corridors, the English furniture and the silver. "My second husband was a prudent man. He never ate meat, rode a stationary bicycle every day, and took handfuls of vitamins." She found him on the floor in the bathroom one summer morning in their house by the sea. She remembers the dead weight of his head when she tried to lift it onto her lap.

"How awful for you," Meg says, putting her hand on Di's arm. "Let's not talk about the past; it's too depressing." Meg lifts her lovely hands in the air with the fingers spread, as though she wishes to keep the past at bay.

Ann rattles ice in her glass and says, "Why do you think Sunny brought us here?"

Di says, "Not to talk about our lives, I hope! Perhaps I came here to see Meg."

Meg says, "I came here to see all of you and to have a good time. Let's do it."

Ann, whose husband is as handsome as he is unfaithful, says, "Oh, for God's sake, Meg! You were always having such a fucking good time, weren't you? It was always such a fucking lovely day."

Mary says sternly to Ann, "It's a question of attitude. Some of us see the glass as half full, others, as half empty."

Ann lifts her gin and tonic and lime and squints at it through her thick glasses in the muted light. "It has been said, of course, that there is no such concept as a thing itself."

Meg, as though suddenly inspired by a deep thought, says, "What do things matter when compared with love?"

Fuzzie leans forward to lift her glass, and for a moment, we see the fat little girl with her shiny tunic stretching across her stomach. She says, "Too much pineapple juice."

No one speaks, but we all remember, surely. We see Di moving through the half dark of the dormitory in her disguise as a man, her painted mustache running into her mouth, a glass of spiked pineapple juice in her hand.

Di rises. Despite her weight and her elegant suit, she swings a long leg easily over the bench. She says she has to "cross the bridge," using the school euphemism, though there is no longer any bridge to cross. We listen to her firm, rapid steps. Meg rises and goes after her, moving smoothly and swiftly, as she always did, in the water and on land, flitting slim and specter-like through the shadows. When they have left the veranda, Ann, too, rises in her crumpled tartan and short-sleeved shirt and walks down the table to Sheila. "Di's husband had just taken out an insurance policy in her name for a million rands, the day before he died. *Et comme c'est étrange et quelle coïncidence,* hey?"

Sheila, who once signed her letters "From an undiscovered genius," has perhaps just had an idea for another book she always wanted to write, for she says, to no one in particular, "I have my work. I do have my work, you know."

The candles are lit

UNDER THE STAR-WILD sky we sit on the long veranda, listening to the myriad sounds of the dusk: rustlings and creakings, chirping of the crickets, a door slamming. Our voices seem to come and then flow away like an echo. There are night-hawks. There is the smell of damp earth and cut grass. There is a slight mist rising low and thin, like gauze in the blue air.

Fuzzie says, "The mosquitoes are attacking my calves and eating me alive."

"Light the camphor candles, please; they'll ward off the mosquitoes," Di orders the ancient servant.

He lights them all along the table, bending over in his wrinkled white uniform, his hands shaking, fumbling with the big box of kitchen matches. He shades the flare of the match from the breeze with one pink-palmed, black hand. The candle flames twist and righten in the air. We lean across the table toward the flames, drawn toward them, as if they could protect us from the dangers of the encroaching dark, and our white faces are brought closer, so that for the first time we form a group again, like people on a dark night on a dark beach, taking their holiday.

Then, half bent, he brings the heavy silver platters, laying them out on the side table. There is a fat brown turkey, its shins frilled and crisp, a great ham, its skin scored and dotted with dark cloves, a whole leg of lamb, cooked English style, dark outside and in. Between the meat and poultry are dishes of roast potatoes, gem squash, butter melting in the scooped-out halves, green beans almondine, mint jelly, and gravy boats, a thin film of fat floating on their surface. There are dishes of custard and pears cooked in red wine and a white, iced granadilla cake on a frilled doily.

We serve ourselves abundantly, refilling our wineglasses, and rising for seconds. Our faces flicker and change in the strange light, as we heap the food high on our plates. There is grease around our mouths, down to our chins; our lips are stained with red wine, our lipstick, smudged, our camouflage, undone. We are transformed, unmasked by the fatigue, the food, the candlelight. The breeze picks up, and the candles send shifting shadows across the table. The stars flame brightly above us. The moon rises.

Someone says, "Remember St. Agnes's Eve?"

Each one remembers the night differently, but vaguely, because we were so drunk. Everyone agrees that no one wanted to hurt Fiamma. We just wanted to have fun with her. We wanted Miss G to have fun with her, too.

We remember with a sense of exhilaration, as though we were once again celebrating an ancient ritual. We laugh, and we feel better. We remember the long, narrow dormitory. We see the Trevelyans embracing, their thin shoulder blades milk white in the moonlight, like wings. We hear Meg and Di make the moans we associated with love.

Fuzzie sits before the low bowl of anemones, which seem to

glimmer mysteriously with the light of their deep reds and purples. They flutter in the breeze, opening and shutting their petals like their sea cousins, drifting back and forth in dark waters, as she sings the pure, clear notes of an ancient madrigal.

How horrible is it?

THE CANDLES burn low. Di has removed her black shantung jacket. Grease marks her blue scarf. She is the only one left eating.

Ann says the worst part of her husband's job is the awful, dull dinners for visiting dignitaries they have to attend. So much wasted food, when so many are starving. She says her politician-husband wants her to buy expensive frocks from the Faubourg St. Honoré to wear at these dinners. But what use would such frocks be on her frumpy figure? Besides, whatever she does, her husband leaves her on the weekends for the village where he was born. He dons the loincloth of his childhood, sits in the dust, and smokes dagga. She would love to go with him, but he does not want her there. "You do not belong," he says.

"The villa is empty as a tomb," Ann says, shuddering.

While the moon slips through clouds, Di finally pushes her dish away and speaks slowly, as though she is regaining her memory. She tells us that the irony is that she threw herself into dance after she left school, although she was too tall. She wanted nothing to do with men, but her first husband told her he found her irresistibly attractive. Perhaps it was her fortune he actually found irresistible, she says, laughing. "One was supposed to marry, wasn't one? Besides, I was pregnant," she says, drinking another glass of red wine, surrounded by the remnants of the huge meal she has consumed.

Fuzzie, resorting to the language of our youth, says, "Do you know, when I got excited, I actually believed I could make myself preggie. All I had to do was cross my legs and shake the bed."

Mary watches Fuzzie sip more wine and says, "You should probably not drink so much, with all the medicine you have to take."

Fuzzie stiffens, and her close-set eyes flash. She says, "I don't feel I need my medicine anymore. I haven't felt so good for years," but she looks at us as though she sees some horror about to surface.

Di says, "At first I thought he might have suffered a slight stroke," referring now to her third and present husband, the German industrialist. "He walks in his sleep. I have to keep my door locked at night, because he once sat on my face and almost suffocated me. He forces me to make love to him in odd ways — he is still a large, strong man. I can hear him shuffling in the acres of corridors, bearing down on me. Can you imagine? He wants me to call him my stallion," Di says, lighting her cigarette. He summons her urgently and has her attend to his needs. He wants her to press her naked back against his fat stomach, while he shouts words at her that she does not understand, words that sound harsh and cruel. She has never managed the language, such a difficult one, she complains, even worse than Afrikaans, which she hated, too. She has to let him clamber up on her back and take her coarse, dyed hair in his hands and yank her head back, while she calls him the German word for stallion, a word she always forgets. Then he pushes and prods into her orifices with his thick, gnarled fingers.

"It is horrible, horrible," Di says, bursting shamelessly into tears, to our utter surprise, and putting her head down in her arms on the trestle table with the bread crumbs, the gravy-stained tablecloth, the empty coffee cups, and the cigarette butts.

"Don't worry," Meg says and puts her hand on Di's arm, but

Meg is weeping, too. She weeps not only for Di, or for her un-born children, but also for Fiamma, who is not here. Di lifts her head, the paint running across her bloated cheeks, as it did years ago. She says, "You understand, because you are good. You would understand, too, Ann, because you understand every-thing. I don't. I only know that everything is gone. It came to an end a long time ago."

Sheila, who lived in France for a while, says, *"Tout passe, tout casse, tout lasse."*

"And what about desire?" Fuzzie says, throwing back her head and laughing, as we all hear the echo of Miss G's exhortation.

We remember the moonlit night when Miss G strode sud-denly into the dormitory. We can still hear her voice calling Fi-amma, and our drunken giggles. We all laugh in the moonlight, our faces glowing. We are suddenly unaccountably lighthearted. A mood of revelry has taken hold of us, as though all this talk has washed us as clean and pure as the light of the moon.

Fuzzie is queen of the May

PAMELA SAYS it is a pity there is no piano out here; Fuzzie could play us a tune. But Di says, "It's late. Let's go to bed," and rises from the bench.

Fuzzie, also rising, recites in her lovely voice:

> You must wake and call me early,
> Call me early, mother dear;
> For I'm to be Queen of the May.

The rest of us rise together and leave the table, going through the hall, hurrying past what had been Miss G's door, like the tide rising, flowing up the dusty stairs, going fast, in silence, along the corridor leading to the dormitory now called Mandela, back to where we slept so many years ago. In the muted light of the corridor our middle-aged faces look gray and worn — even Meg's, her dark curls falling lankly into her slanting, Asian eyes.

She says she remembers how her father used to say they should have named a wing of the school Donovan because of all the tuition he had to pay for his five girls. Meg no longer hears from him. He left her mother for a younger woman soon after her little sister died. "It was too much for him," she says sadly. No one speaks.

We hesitate on the threshold of the dormitory once called Kitchener. No one wants to go in first. Someone turns the brass handle of the door gingerly. Slowly we release the tongue of the lock and open the door onto half darkness. We enter and look into the deeper darkness at the row of neat, narrow beds that await us and the basins that run down the center of the room.

The moon has sunk; all the lights are out. It has begun to rain again, a hard drumming on the roof. A great, dark downpour has begun. In it we all see Fiamma, floating toward us, half naked, the crown of daisies aslant on her forehead, gliding across the parquet, her head slightly to one side, her cheek almost caressing her shoulder, playing "St. Agnes's Eve."

PART FOUR

DISGUISE

✦➤ ✦ ◄✦

Why Miss Nieven called us into her room

O N T H E N I G H T Fiamma disappeared, Miss Nieven called
the twelve of us into her study. We were only summoned
there if we had done something seriously wrong, or if there was
very bad news.

Before we went in, we were told to shower and change our
stained clothes. We were allowed to stay in the shower for as
long as we liked, feeling the water on our bodies. We washed
our hair for the first time in weeks, because of the drought. We
scrubbed. We stared up at the ceiling and thought about Fiamma. We thought of the mosquitoes and the flies — so many
of them; we could still hear the hum.

In the study there were no mosquitoes. The windows were
kept closed, and the heavy red velvet curtains were drawn in the
evening light. We could hear the grandfather clock in the hall
chime the hour, and the wind beat in the palm fronds.

A green-shaded lamp cast a pool of light on the baize of Miss
Nieven's large mahogany desk. Leather-bound books lined the
walls, and a fern grew in a wooden pot. Her personal servant, an
ancient black man in a rumpled white jacket, brought a bulb-

shaped bottle of water and a glass on a silver tray and placed it beside her, slowly and solemnly, as we, too, filed in solemnly.

We sat cross-legged on the red carpet and spoke in hushed voices. We darted quick glances at one another. We looked changed: cleaner, lighter, paler, ashen beneath the eyes.

We floated in the dim light of the room. It was as though we were dreaming, or had left our bodies behind with Fiamma under the frangipanis. We kept seeing the filtered light, the still water, and her clear eyes staring up at us. We huddled close in our thin dresses. We sweated in the thick heat, filled with the coldhearted thrill of tragedy.

Miss Nieven spoke about Fiamma, pulling as usual on the hair that grew from the wart on her chin. We found it hard to pay attention. We shifted about while she stretched out her sentences. She thought she was reassuring us, but she was not.

She told us that she wanted to hear exactly what had happened on the walk. She hoped, she said, that Fiamma would be found before nightfall, that everything was being done to find her, but that, if she were not, and if we did not clear up the mystery, she would be obliged to call in the police.

Search parties had already been sent out. They had dogs with them. They might have to drag the river, but she was still hoping nothing worse than a sprained ankle had befallen Fiamma. There was always the possibility that she might have got lost out there, and that someone would have found her and would call the school at any moment. Her voice trembled as she added that Fiamma was not a very strong girl, with her breathing disorder, nor was she familiar with our veld. She may have underestimated the dangers of the terrain, the wide open spaces, the heat, the monotony of the landscape. She may not have been aware of how easy it was to lose oneself out there.

Fiamma had been protected from danger. She was used to straight paths and gardens with clipped hedges and ancient, shady trees. She might even have fallen asleep in the sun; it might be a case of simple sunstroke. There was no reason to panic, or to think she could have drowned in that little stream, superb swimmer that she was. There was no reason to jump to the worst conclusions.

Nothing like this had happened before at this school. Still, all necessary precautions had to be taken, and it would be very helpful if we would tell her what we knew. We were, after all, not only the last ones to have seen her but also her teammates, were we not? We were likely to know if Fiamma had said anything unusual, if something had upset her, or if she had taken it into her head to go off to telephone her sick father. She was headstrong.

We shifted about and looked at one another and stared blankly. Ann took off her thick glasses to wipe her small, red eyes, and her face looked naked. She was sweating. Two tears ran down her sallow cheeks. Fuzzie whispered to Sheila something about her mother just wanting to grow dahlias and not orchids, but Sheila told her to shut up. Di looked almost green around the lips. She was holding on to Meg's arm so tightly that Meg winced. The Trevelyans said they had to cross the bridge and walked out, holding their stomachs. They looked deathly pale from all the fermented pineapple juice they had drunk the night before.

Miss Nieven said, "Everything will remain between us, *intra muros*. We are all on the same side, after all," whistling again when she pronounced the *s*'s and exposing her row of yellow teeth.

She told us not to try to protect anyone. We knew to whom she was referring: one who had pulled at one cigarette after the other, grinding them out beneath the heel of her boot, whose eyes were as dark as midnight and showed a gleam of terror, a wild hare's look.

Miss Nieven told Di that as captain of the swimming team, she should speak up first. What did she remember about the walk to the river? What had happened in the dormitory, last night?

There was a long silence. The stilled sounds of evening were all that came to us, the sounds of the rain-stunned garden. Di stared ahead. Her deep blue eyes looked black, and her light skin seemed to have lost all its glow. Miss Nieven looked her in the eye and said in a sweet voice, "Well, Diane, what do you have to say?"

Di rose to her feet, and we all turned to look at her. She seemed to have grown ungainly in her height and the heavy muscles of her brown legs. She caught her spill of thin hair and pulled it from her face. She said what we already knew. She said the girls on the swimming team had organized a midnight feast, that we had spent most of the night eating a lot of oily sardines and peaches in sweet syrup, and drinking condensed milk and fermented pineapple juice. Fiamma had had a good time along with the rest of us. No one had slept well after it, because we all felt sick. She said it had started to rain very hard, this afternoon on the walk, and we had taken shelter in the picnic hut. Then the sun had come out again, and there were lots of mossies, and it got very hot. We had last seen Fiamma lying in the shadow of the frangipani trees. She'd seemed quiet and calm. When Miss G had asked if anyone had seen her, we had hunted for her everywhere. Then Miss G had told us to line up, and we had come back to school. Di sat down again, and Ann, who had lost her handkerchief that afternoon, borrowed Di's and blew her nose loudly. Fuzzie let out a little noise that might have been either a giggle or a sob.

We trooped out of the study and stumbled down the wisteria-covered pergola. The school was very quiet, more so than usual for a Sunday evening. The place seemed empty, as if the girls were absent and the constant hum of their voices, silenced. The seringa tree drooped lifelessly over the wooden bench; ivory clouds were pinned to a still blue sky. We listened to the hollow sound of our shoes on stone.

A group of girls was huddling together in the shadows and light of the long pergola. They were whispering. One of them bent down to pull up a brown sock and lifted her head to stare at us, as the others did when we filed past. They went on staring at us sullenly, as we walked down the steps that led into the long, covered corridor. Slowly we descended them, linked like a chain, one after the other.

Whose idea was the feast?

THE IDEA for a midnight feast came to Di after she had seen Miss G and Fiamma together in the changing hut. She immediately told the twins, and they eagerly agreed, because they were always starving, because they did not receive any parcels with extra sweets and biscuits, as everyone else did. Orphans, they sat in agony after each breakfast, hearing the long list of names called out; their names were never called. They did not even receive books about horses. They were always trying to borrow *Thunderhead* or *My Friend Flicka* from Mary, who had the whole series and would part with them only grudgingly, because she was also horse-mad. Sometimes the twins slipped out of their beds at night and went and lay down in the stables on the straw to be near the horses. The smell of manure and sweat, the swish of the tails, the stamping of hooves on the stone floor, a sudden sweet whinnying, comforted them. They were the ones who spiked the pineapple juice by leaving it to ferment for ages under the oak tree by the hockey field.

Di suggested the dancing and the dressing up, because she wanted to dance with Meg in the disguise of a man.

And, certainly, it was Sheila who thought of acting out the roles of all the characters in Keats's poem, which was her favorite. She thought it was brilliant. She said, "Some of us can be Madeline and some, Porphyro. We can dress up and have a beadsman and a beldame. Someone can hobble around."

Mary said, "I'll be Porphyro with his steed," and began rushing around the room, waving an imaginary whip in the air.

Meg murmured, "I will be Madeline and pray for a dream lover in the moonlight," getting down on her knees, spreading her dark curls on her shoulders, and putting her hands together in mock prayer.

Pamela said, "Fiamma can be Madeline, and Miss G can be her Porphyro," and we all clutched at one another feverishly and giggled.

Then Ann recited the part of the poem we liked best:

> Her rich attire creeps rustling to her knees:
> Half-hidden, like a mermaid in sea-weed,
> Pensive awhile she dreams awake, and sees,
> In fancy, fair St. Agnes in her bed,
> But dares not look behind, or all the charm is fled.

St. Agnes's Eve

> Fuzzie sang songs of long ago.
> Ann recited to the moon.
> Never before had Fiamma feasted so,
> While we, in lovers' arms, swooned.

> We drank, we ate, we discarded our clothes
> The moon shone on our flesh.
> We lay together, we dreamed of love,
> We lost ourselves, enmeshed.

W E HAD NEVER seen Fiamma have as much fun as she did
the night before she disappeared. It was the same for
most of us. We liked the food, the dressing up and pretending,
the drink, the excitement, and the dreams of love in the moonlight. The languid moonlight advanced, as we lay side-by-side
in the dormitory, trying to stay awake until midnight.

We waited up impatiently with the windows and curtains
open. We sweated in the heat. Some of us hid in the bathrooms,
reading our books to pass the time and swatting at the mosquitoes, jumping up to kill them with our slippers, the blood
marking the walls. We listened to the grandfather clock in the
hall chime midnight. Then we rose and slipped down to fetch
the flowers from the bathroom under the stairs.

Miss G had suggested we ask Fiamma to help decorate the
dormitory with the flowers: "You know, Fiamma is wonderful
with flowers." When we told her what we were planning, Miss
G's eyes had turned brilliant, and she had said longingly. "Italians are very artistic. They have the imagination, the flair. They
are full of surprises." Then she had brought forth the business
about no repression of libidinal urges and how repression led to
aggression and told us to let our imaginations soar, our emo-
tions rule our hearts.

And to our surprise Fiamma had acquiesced, rising oblig-
ingly from her bed and mixing goldenrod with lavender in big
jars by the windows. We discovered her gift with her hands that
night. When she had finished with the flowers, she piled up
fruit and tins of sardines in the basins along the center of the
dorm. Finally, she helped us with our disguises.

Naturally, Ann was designated as our reader. She perched in
the windowsill with her torch, intoning the lilting verses of
"The Eve of St. Agnes" in her monotonous, nasal voice and
blowing her nose from time to time. While she read, we acted

out the poem: we ate and drank and discarded our clothes as Madeline does, before we climbed into our beds to wait for our imaginary lovers. We hid behind doors or under our beds in the role of the real lover, Porphyro.

Di, in her panama hat, tilted at a rakish angle, and galoshes, danced up and down the dormitory with Meg, holding her around the waist and turning her around and around. Fuzzie sang madrigals with flowers in her red curls. The Trevelyans shimmied around the dormitory completely naked, hugging one another like lovers, their thin shoulder blades like white wings in the moonlight.

By the end of the feast we were all wandering about half naked, our makeup smudged, crushed flowers in our loose hair. We were drunk on the juice and wine. We sweated and giggled and sighed, playing the lovers in one another's beds. Then the batteries on Ann's torch failed, and she had to stop reading the poem.

What many of us were to remember best was the white, full disk of the moon. There was thunder and lightning, but no rain. Fuzzie, who was always particularly sensitive to smells, was to remember those of the flowers, mingled with those of hot, sweating bodies, which increased as the night went on.

Why the game of St. Agness's Eve?

> Our robes drifted to our knees.
> Half-hidden like mermaids in seaweed,
> We dreamed awake and saw
> In fancy, Miss G, fairest of all.

"THE EVE OF ST. AGNES" was our favorite poem, although, or perhaps because, Miss Lacey had said we would do much better to read Milton's "Samson Agonistes." Of course, our feast did not take place on St. Agnes's Eve. We did not know when that holiday was. Ann maintained it was probably in December or, anyway, sometime in midwinter, because the poem speaks of such bitter cold. Now it was midsummer for us, and thus the appropriate time.

We wanted, insofar as possible, to make the feast resemble the one in the poem. We wanted to have the same sort of food — the candied apple, the quince, the plum, but in the end all we could procure was the usual midnight feast food: tins of condensed milk and sardines and peaches in sweet syrup. Of course, we had no beadsman, no beldame; we had no Porphyros for our Madelines, but we made believe.

When the detective asked us about the feast, we told him about the food and the alcohol, but no one mentioned Di jumping out of the cupboard in her galoshes and painted mustache and panama hat and not much else, in her role of Porphyro, and climbing into bed with Meg, where they made the sorts of noises they associated with love. No one spoke of passing the pineapple juice to Fiamma, or of her drifting drunkenly around the dormitory, stumbling blindly into the basins in the center of the room.

No one mentioned Miss G.

Who was invited to the feast and why?

ONLY THE GIRLS on the swimming team were invited, naturally. We were all there: Fuzzie, her sheet slipping down her plump, shiny hips, and her daisy chain tilting into her eyes as she sang madrigals; Pamela, half asleep in pajamas tied with a belt around her thin waist, eating peaches, the syrup dripping down her arm; Ann, sitting up in the window seat with her yellow torch and her thick glasses, her collarbones protruding from the sheet tied around her neck, blowing her nose; Di, in pajamas and galoshes, sporting a painted mustache; Meg with a scarf tied tightly across the lilt of her full breasts, lisping softly in Di's ear; the Trevelyans in nothing at all; Lizzie, elegant in white pajamas; Mary in her riding boots and plumed hat, pretending to be Porphyro arriving at the castle on his wild steed "with heart on fire"; and Sheila, spending her time eating tinned sardines and dreaming of love and death.

What Fiamma did at the feast

> Around a neck a knot she ties,
> She drapes a sheet around.
> While her loss draws nigh
> With daisy chains we are bound.

NONE OF US KNEW exactly what cards Fiamma was playing at the midnight feast. We do know that we asked her to join in with us, and to our surprise she did so with enthusiasm. Perhaps she had simply been waiting to be asked, or perhaps the dressing up made her think of her father, who was still languishing in some small hospital somewhere, suffering from increasingly high fever, Miss G said.

Fiamma told us that her father had once taken her to Venice during the carnival season. Everyone dressed up in costumes with masks, so that no one could tell who they were. They had kept their costumes a secret even from one another. Fiamma had made her own costume. She had dressed up as a mermaid with a wonderful tail and mask, and in the crowd of people and the confusion, her father had asked her to dance, not knowing who she was.

Fiamma threw herself into our preparations. She used our sheets, blankets, and scarves to make us look like knights and ladies from long ago. She draped our sheets around us, tied scarves around our heads, and threaded a flower through a plait, standing back to survey her handiwork critically. Instead of jewelry she used the flowers we had stolen from the cutting garden and hidden in the bathroom under the stairs. She made flower chains for our ankles and wrists and foreheads, splitting the stems with a knife and linking them together.

She made up our faces so that we hardly recognized one another. She outlined our eyes with dark pencil and flecked our cheeks with gold paint, so that those of us who were playing Madeline looked like angels. The Porphyros — usually the taller girls: Di, Mary, Pamela, and Lizzie — wore pajama trousers and loose shirts and raked panama hats and, sometimes, galoshes or boots. Fiamma painted their upper lips with black pencil to make them look like men. Like a magician she transformed us. We felt like the inhabitants of some strange, distant land, and in our anonymity and the half dark of our dormitory, we could do anything, say anything, be anything we wanted. We were wild and free. Afterward, because of the heat and sweat, much of the makeup ran, streaking our faces like those of savages.

Fiamma, too, was transformed. We would always remember her, pretending to be the beadsman, telling her rosary on her knees and shivering with cold in the hot dormitory. She looked suddenly old, her smooth brow wrinkled, as though her whole life had passed her by, and she had become the ancient beldame, hobbling blindly down the moonlit dormitory, leaning on a stick for a cane and warning an imaginary Porphyro of the dangers in the house.

> Saying, "Mercy, Porphyro! hie thee from this place:
> They are all here to-night, the whole blood-thirsty race!"

Other staff members who knew about the feast

WE FOUND OUT afterward that Miss Lacey was awakened by the noise. She told Sheila, her favorite, that she had heard a noise coming from Kitchener, but she remembered the midnight feasts of her own youthful schooldays and smiled indulgently, thinking we should be allowed some freedom — after all, this was not the Middle Ages. She decided it was better not to interfere.

The night watchman, John Mazaboko, the tall Zulu from Natal, who was later to die tragically in his room in a fire, said he heard a noise coming from Kitchener but considered it was not his role, a black night watchman in a white girls' school, to report on them.

He also heard footsteps in the very early hours of the morning, when the sky was a faint pink. He was wandering up and down the gravel path under the ancient oaks, the light of his torch punching holes through the dark of the hydrangeas. He looked up and saw a blond girl wrapped in a striped towel, drifting toward the pool in the dawn light.

He said that he called out, "*Sala khale,*" the Zulu greeting, telling her to go carefully, but when she did not respond, he did not follow her, because he, too, had been drinking skokiaan to pass the interminable hours of the empty night, and he thought he might have seen a ghost.

What Miss G did at the feast

NONE OF US had ever seen Fiamma drink so much. She drank from the tin of condensed milk, the thick liquid trickling down her chin. She drank glass after glass of the spiked pineapple juice, which the Trevelyans passed her. She drank the white wine mixed with red that Miss G had provided. She broke a glass, and we had to try to scoop up the pieces with our bare hands in the half-light so that no one would cut her bare feet.

The Trevelyans said afterward that they'd heard what no one else had, a first soft knock on the door, and they said that when they heard it, they had a feeling of anticipation and dread. They feared that it would all end badly.

Then there was a louder knock, which everyone heard. We all kept very still, and some of us, who were naked, crouched down behind the basins, which Fiamma had filled with food and which were now almost empty. The door opened slowly, and Miss G appeared. She loomed, barefooted in her jumpsuit, a long, dark shadow in the light from the corridor. She shut the door behind her quickly and stood there, legs apart, hands on her hips, staring at the disorderly scene in the moonlight. We were all standing around drunkenly, half naked, linked in pairs, flowers in our loose hair, or false mustaches running into our mouths.

She called for Fiamma. She called again, and Fiamma emerged slowly from the shadows. She tottered forward, or perhaps Bobby Joe pushed her, though Bobby Joe denied it later. Bobby Jean, who became a social worker, said she saw her twin pull Fiamma from beside the bed where she was hiding when Miss G called for her. Then Fiamma floated forward. Everyone else was too drunk to speak.

We did recall that Fiamma had remained half naked since early in the evening. Her sheet had slipped down to her waist, baring her full, white bosoms. Her hair was loose. Her crown of daisies tilted across her brow into one eye. Her gold eye shadow was smudged, her lipstick, spread wide like a clown's. Like all of us she smelled of alcohol and sweat.

We moved away from her, as Miss G strode toward her and grabbed her by the arm and held her close as though she were smelling her. She placed her hands on Fiamma's shoulders and looked into her eyes. Then she picked up a scarf that had fallen to the floor and slung it around Fiamma's neck like a halter. "Now you come with me," she said and led her away like a horse. Fiamma stumbled forward blindly. We watched in amazement as the door opened, and they disappeared into the garish neon light.

It was after Fiamma had gone that the batteries in Ann's torch went dead, and only moonlight remained. We clasped one another deliriously in it; we stroked one another's skin, our soft new breasts; we rolled around in one another's beds and pretended to be Fiamma and Miss G and made the sorts of noises we hoped they were making at last.

PART FIVE

DISAPPEARANCE

→►◄←

What happened on the day of
Fiamma's disappearance

ON THE DAY Fiamma was to disappear, she rose at dawn to swim. Ann saw her sit up in her bed in the silence of the sleeping dormitory. In the faint light she already looked like a specter in her soft, long-sleeved nightdress that she had washed, despite regulations, so that the school soap would not aggravate her sensitive skin. Her heavy hair was plaited down her back in a long, limp rope. She told Ann, speaking softly so as not to awaken the others, she had dreamed that she was swimming through the still, trapped water of her lake at home, the mist rising from its gray surface. She felt her body buoyed up by the water and slowly spinning free, escaping into the cool air. She rose, she soared. But when she awoke under her white sheet, she was soaked with sweat.

Ann had acquired a reputation as a remarkable interpreter of dreams, because she had read Freud's dream book, but she did not attempt to interpret that one.

Fiamma said that she had hardly slept, but she was going swimming. Ann reminded her it was Sunday, and she was not supposed to practice but to dress for chapel. Miss G would not be up this early, anyway. "I need to cool off," Fiamma said.

Ann watched her remove her nightdress and wander around the disarrayed dormitory, already hot, though not as hot as it was to become that day. Adorned only with the camphor bag, which trailed on the end of a string, bouncing against her back, she skated her hand across the identical iron bed ends, lined up side-by-side, looking for her racing costume. Her once-proud step, arched and smooth, as if she had never worn shoes, seemed to Ann to have lost its spring. She picked her way with the blank gaze of the sleepwalker, lips slightly parted.

Ann couldn't help staring at her firm white bosoms, the smooth swell of her stomach. She felt the affliction of her own bony body, thick neck, protruding collarbones, shortsightedness. She imagined Fiamma on her hands and knees, begging for mercy.

Fiamma stepped unsteadily into her thin, black racing costume. She tied a striped towel about her waist and picked up her green plastic cap by the buckle from a heap of dead flowers.

Fiamma said nothing about the events of the night before as she walked slowly barefooted past Ann, along the length of the dormitory called Kitchener, now looking like a trash heap, and out the door into the gold light of the early December morning.

In chapel that day

TWELVE OF THE thirteen girls on Miss G's team trooped in late for Sunday chapel. Fiamma was not among us. Ann had promised Fiamma that she would wait for her at the door, but when she did not arrive, Ann came in with the rest of us. We stumbled in one behind another, our hatted heads bent. We were all still dazed; we floated up the blue velvet carpet that lines the center aisle, sweating, light-headed, dry-mouthed, and nauseated.

The twins, who had been up later than anyone, had come in through the side door and were still clumsily arranging the carnations, lilies, and baby's breath in two identical silver flutes on the altar. As scholarship girls, they were made to perform certain functions in the school, despite their lack of artistic ability.

Fuzzie was playing "All Things Bright and Beautiful" on the upright piano, using the damper pedal for dramatic effect, and thumping loudly. Usually, we would make the sign for the organ grinder behind her back, but today we were not doing so; from the corners of our eyes we were watching Miss G's entrance.

She strode down the aisle, her long arms swinging martially at her sides. Her sable eyes blazed, and she held her head high, tipped by her aquiline nose. Like the prow of a ship she dipped and rose proudly over the waves. Her tanned skin glowed. She stirred us with the rustle of her impeccably starched jumpsuit and the triumphant creak of her highly polished boots. She was no longer scratching with the tips of her blunt fingers, and we stopped scratching, too. She had regained her exciting air of recklessness.

The rest of the staff filed in at a distance from her, as usual. They came in pairs, hands folded and heads bowed demurely, in belted cotton dresses of pale pastel colors: mauve, light blue, and beige; Mrs. Willis wore gray, as if to match her skin, discolored from smoking too many cigarettes.

The teachers slipped silently into their places in the chapel pews and sank with a sigh of soft dresses onto their knees, burying their pale faces in their arms or hiding them in their hands. Miss G sat on the other side of the aisle from them, head back, one leg crossed over the other, one arm dangling irreverently over the back of the pew.

What happened to Fiamma in chapel

W E HEARD a great clatter at the back of the church, and the whole school turned around with a rustle of starched white Sunday dresses, sounding like a wave breaking on the shore. "I heard her swear under her breath, saying something in Italian that sounded like a curse," Fuzzie told us afterward. Fiamma was at the back door of the chapel, looking very pale, pumping her inhaler for breath and, when she had regained it, crossing herself, as she deep-curtsied in the aisle.

We had just sat down after singing to Fuzzie's accompaniment when Fiamma came in and knocked a heavy hymnbook onto the floor from the table that stood between the two back doors.

She slid into the last pew and sat beside Di, who rose to her full height and moved further along so that Fiamma would be sitting at the end of the pew, beside Ann. We turned around to catch a glimpse of Fiamma as she sat down, an expression of defiance on her face.

She said nothing to Ann, who moved slightly away from her as well, sliding onto the blue kneeler for the prayer.

While we sang "Ride On! Ride On in Majesty," Fiamma grew increasingly pale, and even Ann's sallow skin looked rosy beside hers. Then we heard a dull thud, as Fiamma slumped forward in the pew and her head struck the wood. She had never fainted before — never made herself faint for Miss G the way we all had done — but she fainted that Sunday morning. Perhaps she did not make herself faint at all; perhaps she just fainted.

Miss Nieven, who was at that moment climbing the steps to

take up her high position in the granite pulpit for her sermon, glanced back on hearing the thud, clasping her ivory-backed prayerbook to her flat spinster breast, as if she would rush down from the stone steps to assist the Princess. But we heard the squelch of Miss G's crepe soled boots as she strode fast along the blue-carpeted aisle to rescue Fiamma. Miss G stood over Fiamma possessively and glared about with a look which was both menacing and aghast.

It was Fiamma whom Miss G rescued on the Sunday Fiamma disappeared.

Our hearts fluttered, as we watched Miss G making Fiamma put her head down between her knees and then leading her down the aisle, her head drooping limply onto Miss G's shoulder, feeling Miss G's breath on her cheek, the soft swell of her boosie, we could see. We saw the light streaming in aslant through the narrow stained-glass windows: red and blue and yellow, like a rainbow.

Miss G led Fiamma out into the cool of the garden, and Fiamma sat on the whitewashed wall under the loquat tree in her white Sunday dress and undid the mother-of-pearl button at her neck, we all imagined, as we stood to say the Nicene Creed. *I believe in God the Father, and God the son,* we intoned, thinking of Miss G sitting on the wall beside Fiamma and smoking a cigarette, holding it under her hand, so Miss Nieven would not notice if she came upon her suddenly. When Miss G told Fiamma to, she must have taken off her panama hat and set it down on the wall. Fiamma must have leaned her head against Miss G's shoulder. It was Fiamma who got to sit there under the cool dark leaves of the loquat tree and feel the breeze lift the hem of her tunic very gently and watch Miss G blow smoke rings, until she asked if Fiamma felt all right now, in her deep hoarse man's voice.

On the front steps

ON THE AFTERNOON Fiamma disappeared we were told to gather on the front steps of the Dutch-gabled school building. We milled around on the red, polished front steps where the two friable sandstone lions stood, and still stand, like sentinels.

Our heads throbbed, and we were nauseated. The twins threw up in the hydrangeas, then sprawled on the steps, their knees apart, wiping the spittle from their wide mouths and holding their flat foreheads in their hands. The sickly scent hung in the heavy air.

The sun disappeared behind clouds, but it was still hot. The oak trees dipped down, dark and heavy. There was a whine of mosquitoes, and from time to time a hand slapped against an arm or a leg, catching a slow one. We waited to line up, grumbling about having to go off on a walk in the early afternoon, rather than being allowed to plunge into the cool of the pool, just because of reports of a thundershower and the other teachers' fears of lightning. Usually, Miss G would shield us from their fears, but not today. Perhaps it was Miss G herself who had suggested this walk.

No one knew why we were kept waiting so long in the heat before starting on the walk. Perhaps, had we left sooner, nothing more would have occurred.

Preparations for a walk

EVEN WITH THE CLOUD cover it was getting hotter by the minute. We sweated in our earth-colored tunics, our heavy lace-up shoes. We were trying to shake off the aftereffects of the midnight feast: the sardines floating in oil, the peaches swimming in syrup, the spiked pineapple juice. We were thinking of Fiamma fainting in chapel.

Meg said her mother had often fainted when she was preggie. One time Meg saw her mother fall down from the table where she was turning around, having a hem pinned up. Perhaps that was Fiamma's problem, Meg lisped. Ann told her not to be so dumb: Fiamma had not even got the curse, so how could she possibly be preggie?

Fuzzie said, "Maybe, if you do it with another woman in the dark, you can get preggie." Ann told her not to be so absurd, that you needed a man, obviously.

"Well, she could have been more of a sport and waited a couple of weeks before taking her turn to faint; she was just showing off, again," Di said, scornfully.

"And did you see how she upset Miss G?" Mary added.

Fiamma at last sauntered up and sprawled alone in silence in the shadows of the lions on the last step of the Dutch-gabled building. She sat, tracing letters in the dust with the end of a stick and then erasing them with her lace-up shoe. No one sat near her. Ann remained perched on the step above Sheila and began reading *The Life of Charlotte Brontë* by Gaskell in a small, blue, leather-backed volume Sheila had lent her.

We grew silent when Miss G approached.

Miss G and Fiamma

WE TURNED QUIET as Miss G came striding through a side door in her usual uniform of crepe-soled boots and khaki jumpsuit. She stood before us; she looked up the stairs. Her clothes were as neat as ever, her boots as highly lacquered, but, for the first time, Miss G's eyes were shaded from the glare and from us by small, round, wire-rimmed sunglasses. The glasses glinted at us ominously in the glare. She asked us what we were waiting for, kingdom come? Why had we not lined up by now? She told us to hurry up and get lined up two by two. We could see she was in an anxious mood.

Miss G strode over to Fiamma and bent toward her and asked her something, probably if she was feeling better. Fiamma slumped sulkily in the shadows. She traced letters in the sand, her head slightly to one side, her skin so white and her hair so pale she looked almost as though she did not exist. She did not bother to look up. We heard her say quite clearly in her bored, truculent tone that she was suffering from pains. Miss G bent her head down further and whispered something softly. She must have told her to hush.

There was a pause, a moment of silence. We all looked at one another, raised our eyebrows, goggled our eyes. Miss G crouched down beside Fiamma; she put her arm around her shoulder, and whispered in her ear. We could see there was more than longing in Miss G's eyes now; there was fear. Cajoling, we could see, Miss G was cajoling; she was making promises. She was placating. She was making jokes. She was trying to make Fiamma smile.

But Fiamma did not smile. She did not even pay attention to Miss G. Fiamma was enjoying her moment of power, we were sure. Instead the same distant look came over her face as it had the first time we had seen her in the dormitory. She seemed to look through Miss G, as though she did not recognize her, or as though she were not there, as though Fiamma were staring at the hydrangea bushes behind her where the Trevelyan twins had vomited.

Fiamma flicked her pale plait back from her shoulder and looked around distractedly. She rose and walked away from Miss G slowly in her careless way and went toward Ann, but Ann already had a partner. Ann was standing next to Mary Skeen, so Fiamma was obliged to follow along at the end of the line, alone.

The walk itself

There was nothing but heat
And above, the white sky.
We did not know whom we would meet
Or where Fiamma was to lie.

WE FOLLOWED Miss G down the driveway in silence. The sun had softened the recently tarred surface, and our heavy lace-up shoes pressed into it. We smelled the tar, as we walked, two-by-two, through the iron gates and across the veld. We stumbled on in our dark brown tunics. We were lost out there. There was nothing to see except dull fields and a sky, scattered with an occasional cloud, black-bellied and bulbous, and in the distance a shimmer of heat.

The light, the odors, the fatigue, the nausea, the memories of the night before — flashes of white flesh in the moonlight, Miss G standing with the scarf like a halter around Fiamma's neck, made it hard for us to think straight. Occasionally, one of us dropped down into the long grass and wriggled forward in the dust on our stomach and elbows, playing Red Indians, as we had done as small children. The twins and Mary started to play horsie, but Miss G soon put a stop to childish games. Fiamma dragged her feet at the end of the line. She looked sullen, with her pouting mouth.

Miss G suddenly burst into song. She had a sweet Welsh voice that her strong appearance belied. As she sang, she swung her arms. She recovered more and more of the bounce in her step as we went along, going farther and farther from the school into the wilderness. She strode on beside us, hatless, slim, and strong. She looked brave and beautiful. Behind her dark head the sky seemed whiter. We took it all in: the vast sky, the gray branches of a dead tree, the silver wattle leaves scintillant in the valley, the low, blue hills crouched menacingly in the distance.

We, too, swung our arms, as we attempted to march as straight as she, picking up our step. We sang lustily, tears in our eyes, moved by the sound of her alto voice and by the words of the hymn, which was her, and therefore our, favorite hymn. She lifted her head, and her voice rang out to the horizon:

> Bring me my Bow of burning gold:
> Bring me my Arrows of desire:
> Bring me my Spear: O Clouds unfold!
> Bring me my Chariot of fire.

Even Meg Donovan sang our Protestant hymn, as we strode across the dry veld. The only one not singing was Fiamma. She was dragging her feet in silence, flicking her long plait back from her face. She looked sulky and disconsolate. She pumped her inhaler, breathing loudly and coughing her shallow cough. She was not sweating like the rest of us, and her face was pale.

Miss G glanced back at her from time to time, and when she did so, we could see the dark turmoil in her face. She interrupted her singing to encourage Fiamma onward.

"Why do you want to go so far in this beastly heat?" Fiamma asked in a loud voice. But Miss G pressed forward, as though there were some urgent purpose to our march.

When we looked back we could see Fiamma receding slowly, dissolving in the haze of heat and dust. She was farther and farther behind. We realized she must have stopped dead in her tracks. Miss G halted the march.

Her face was as somber as the clouds above us. We watched her stride back to Fiamma, a frail, flickering figure in the heat, standing in the dusty tracks, her head hanging on her chest. We could see from the way Fiamma waved her slender arms and hands about that she was objecting to going further. Miss G was exhorting Fiamma onward. We stood in a silent crescent, watching the drama unfold, waiting. We saw Miss G put her hand to her wire-rimmed glasses to slide them down her nose, we presumed, to make Fiamma look her in the eye. They returned to us together.

When we approached the shade trees along the banks of the river, we broke ranks before being told to do so. We rushed impulsively toward the water, pulling off our shoes, tucking up our tunics, and scrambling down the bank. We waded in; we splashed one another's hot faces; we skipped over the burning stones. Fuzzie slipped and fell in the gray mud and had to be helped to her feet.

We watched Fiamma stroll off downstream. No one followed. From a distance we saw her bend over, staring at her reflection in the water. It appeared that she was trying to splash some of the cool water up between her legs.

What we remember most clearly about that afternoon

THE HEAT and the mosquitoes and the flies. The flies were black and iridescent green and numberless. They alighted on our sweating flesh; they tickled; they gorged; they bit.

The stench of the latrines.

The disk of the sun, a dull silver. The stifling air in the valley. The hot air seemed white.

The afternoon wore on, hazy and dreadful with damp heat. The air was as heavy as steam on our faces. It was too hot to climb up the bank again. We all stayed down at the edge of the water, our heads pounding with the sun, the aftereffects of the alcohol, the lack of sleep. Our mouths were dry; our temples pulsed. Mosquitoes buzzed around our ankles and our calves. We kept moving slowly, driven onward by the heat, the mosquitoes, the flies, the dullness of the long Sunday afternoon. We all sauntered along the bank chewing on pieces of grass, arms thrown loosely around one another's waists or shoulders, smacking at mosquitoes, wiping the sweat from our brows, our shadows mingling.

There was nothing to do.

Di, with her arm slung lazily around Meg's shoulder, walked in front; the Trevelyan twins, arms around one another's waists, followed. Then came Ann, walking beside Mary and Sheila and Pamela, with Ann sucking on the end of a piece of grass and holding forth about the dangers of polio and the risks of contagion in our school. Lizzie, pale and alone, her hair tied back neatly in a ponytail, walked behind; and, coming last, picking her way with her soft-soled feet and her odd, catlike walk and complaining, Fuzzie, saying she had a terrible headache and was particularly hot because of the vest her dead mother had told her to wear at all times and because the mosquitoes were attacking her.

From time to time thunder struck in the distance. Fuzzie limped and called out, "I wish it would rain."

"It will never rain again," Sheila predicted, turning her head and speaking over her shoulder.

None of us could think clearly because of the heat and our hangovers and the muffled boom of thunder. Our minds were blank in the glare.

We inched forward slowly, sweating in the silence and the heat, drawn by a strange sort of curiosity toward the rock where Fiamma lay in the shade of the wattles and the willows that leaned down over the water. From that distance she was a blur of white and pink. "Do you think she might tell on Miss G?" Meg asked Ann.

"If she is given a chance, in all probability she will," Ann said.

What we were thinking on the bank of the river

MEG WAS STILL feeling sick from all the sweet peaches swimming in syrup and the sardines floating in oil. As she walked in the shadows of the wattles along the bank of the river toward Fiamma, she remembered the afternoon when she had told Miss G about her father beating her and her sisters, when Miss G had responded by touching her knee, making everything swing around her.

Di walked by the bank of the river and remembered a game she and her sister had played when they were very young. They rolled down the bank with their hands over their heads and their eyes shut, rolling over and over down the bank, helplessly.

Sheila wanted something exciting to happen, at that moment. She imagined someone might drown accidentally, or be struck by lightning, just to relieve the boredom of the afternoon.

Fuzzie walked along the bank and remembered the voices she had heard as a lonely child. She was afraid she might hear them again. She felt as though her heart had escaped her; she could feel it beating steadily, but it felt like someone else's heart, not hers.

Fiamma among the wattles

WE ALL ADVANCED toward Fiamma in silence, a compact group, our shadows mingling. We saw things obscurely through the tremble of the heat and the steamy air. There was little sign of the approaching storm now, apart from the continuous growl of thunder. The riverbanks were swept clean, like scoured blades; the trees cast somber shadows. Reflected in the surface of the water were the heavy sky, the clouds, the occasional swallows, dipping down around us.

Fiamma was still stretched out on the gray rock in the shade of the wattles. We were moving toward her slowly. Wild white irises grew nearby, and bright butterflies danced around one another over her head. One hand trailed in the water, the other, behind her head. Her legs looked very pale and slim. She seemed asleep or, at least, content and calm. The only thing moving was the hem of her dress, fluttered by a faint breeze.

When she felt us draw near, she sat up and looked at us. She put her hand to her eyes to shield them from the sun.

We all stood there in the silence by the river.

She said, "What are you all staring at, anyway?"

It was then that we got the idea: "Let's play the game of truth!"

Di Radfield and Miss G

MISS G STRODE through the wattles, snapping the twigs beneath the soles of her boots. Her impeccably ironed jumpsuit rustled, and her round glasses glinted once again. "Come with me, Radfield," she called out imperiously.

Miss G offered her a cigarette. They went off for a smoke all on their own. We watched them go together, whispering. Miss G had never allowed anyone to smoke with her before. She had always forbidden it. For years afterward Di could remember the taste of that cigarette.

They sat under the wattles, smoking and watching the dragonflies skim over the water. Di did not really like it; it made her feel sick, particularly because she was already feeling so, but after that day she took it up: she kept reaching for another.

They dipped their hands into the water. Miss G had often told her, before Fiamma's arrival, that she was the best swimmer on the team, the strongest, the most enduring, but that day, while they were smoking, Miss G told her that she should know the truth. Di already knew what she was going to say, which was that Fiamma was a much better swimmer than Di would ever be, that Fiamma would always beat her in the end, that what Di had was simply endurance, but that Fiamma had it all.

"She's the real thing," Miss G told Di, while the sun beat

down on the gray water, and Di learned to pull hard on a cigarette and then stub it out beneath the heel of her shoe.

Rain

O N THE DECEMBER DAY Fiamma disappeared, it rained
for the first time in months. We could hardly remember
the last time. It suddenly started raining hard while we were
down by the river, and we had to take shelter in the picnic hut.
It was because of the rain that we came to play the game of
truth with Fiamma.

We heard it in the leaves before we felt it, a rustling, like the
wind. Then everything came on very fast. The clouds opened,
and a waterfall descended on us. The wind picked up so hard, it
blew the water sideways. The big drops became hailstones that
came down brutally, like grapeshot. Lightning forked across the
sky, scattering us. Some ran, screaming, to shelter under the
nearest trees; some rushed into the thatched picnic hut, which
was set up below the graves by the side of the river with a few
rickety wooden tables and benches and a beaten-earth floor.

The two privies, deep holes in the earth infested with flies,
were at the back. Their stench was barely mitigated by the smell
of lime, and when it rained, it became overpowering.

The hail continued to pound down steadily on the thatched
roof, while we huddled at the tables. We listened and watched
the red earth spatter, forming deep pools, and played the game
of truth. We wanted Fiamma to tell us what had happened with
Miss G the night before.

Where was Miss G?

N O ONE WAS SURE exactly where Miss G had gone after Di came back to us. She seemed to have vanished with the coming of rain. When Fuzzie asked after her, Meg said she had seen her go to the privy, that she must have been in there all the while, but we could not imagine how anyone could have shut herself up there for so long. Pamela said she thought she had fallen asleep at the back of the picnic hut, where she had heard heavy breathing. Fuzzie said she was certain that she had smelled smoke while we were playing. Afterward we thought she might very well have been sitting at the back, listening and watching, able to overhear the rude things Fiamma was saying.

Fiamma resisted playing the game with us, but not for the reason we had expected: she was not interested in keeping her secret; she wanted us to know what she had done for us, but she no longer thought of it as a game. Nothing obliged her to say what she did. Afterward we wondered what Miss G must have thought, if she had overheard us.

Fuzzie said, "Perhaps Fiamma had always wanted to play with us, and she was just doing her Princess act and waiting to be asked."

The game of truth

I T WAS ANN'S TURN on the sidelines. It was she who caught Fiamma with her hand at the bottom of the pile. We held Fiamma's hand down, so she would have to answer the question.

Ann looked at Fiamma, and her small red eyes shimmered behind her glasses in the shadows of the picnic hut. We could hear the hail beating down on the thatched roof as Ann asked Fiamma, "What happened with Miss G last night? Why do you have pains? Are you bleeding?"

Fuzzie said, "You are only supposed to ask her one question."

Fiamma said nothing. There was a long silence as we all stared at Fiamma and waited. We could hear her shallow, ragged breathing and saw her hand going to her pocket for her inhaler. Meg clutched the little camphor bag around her neck and asked, "Did you play St. Agnes's Eve with Miss G?"

Bobby Joe put up her hands in prayer and made little kissing movements with her lips.

We all laughed.

Fiamma took out her inhaler and pumped.

The hail was coming down hard as stones, tearing at the wild irises that grew along the bank of the river, the low scrub, and the thatched roof of the picnic hut. We all gathered around Fiamma, listening to the hail and smelling the latrines and the wet earth and the faint odor of smoke. The red mud was running down the bank to the river, while we were laughing and making kissing noises and waiting for Fiamma's reply. After a while Di said, "You have to answer," and we all took it up, clapping and chanting, "Answer, answer, answer. Give us the truth, Princess Fiamma! Princess Fiamma!" Fiamma sat in silence, looking stiff and bored and watching the hail fall.

Sheila asked, "Why did you faint in chapel this morning?"

Fiamma said, "I told you. I have pains," and she got up and tried to walk out of the circle, but we were barring her way. We pulled at her tunic; we grabbed at her legs; Di got up and pushed on her shoulders; we made her sit down. Besides, there was nowhere to go in the rain. "Not so fast, Princess Fiamma.

Sit down, sit down," Di said. Fiamma sat. She crossed her arms. She scowled.

Di said, "You have to tell us what happened last night. It's the rule of the game."

Fiamma sat cross-legged, her head held high. She said, "What do you think happened?"

Ann said, "Did you *do* it with Miss G? Did you do it for *real*? Is that why you're in pain?"

Di asked, "You're not a *virgin* anymore?"

Meg said, "You actually did it with *Miss G?*" and pulled her mouth down in a grimace of disgust.

Fiamma looked at us with her blank stare. She looked very bored and tired, and she pulled at the end of her plait. There were dark circles under her eyes, and her breathing was fast and shallow. She said, "I did what you asked me to do."

Meg said, "But we just asked you to be *nice.*"

Di, who had confessed to letting a boy put his finger up her winkie, said, "You were a *lezzie* with Miss G? Yuck. *Disgusting,*" and sounded as if she were going to be sick.

Fuzzie said, "You played Madeline and Porphyro *for real* with Miss G?"

Fiamma shrugged her shoulders and said in her low, slow voice, "Oh, grow up, all of you, can't you?" She put her hand to her pocket again, searching for her inhaler, and said in a loud, firm voice, "Someone should report your Miss G to the authorities. Someone should close this prison down. I'm going to make sure my father hears about all of this."

Di said, "But Miss G thinks you are the best."

Fiamma looked around at us with her clear gaze. She pumped and said, "And I am the best."

We were all gathered around by now, smelling blood. Everyone drew closer, elbowing Fuzzie out of the way. The hail stopped suddenly, or perhaps it had stopped earlier, and we had not noticed. The breeze had died, too. There was the strong scent of wet earth and wet grass and the rising stench from the latrines, the smell of smoke. It was very quiet again; all we could hear was Fiamma's ragged breathing and the screaming of the cicadas. Fiamma looked down, and her face seemed to reflect the color of the beaten red earth. Then she looked up at us. She said, "Don't you understand? Miss G doesn't tell you the truth. She tells you what you want to hear, what is convenient for her. She's not all that powerful. No one learned to swim or do anything else by *desiring* it. You either know how to, or you don't. I happen to know how, and you don't."

Miss G's reaction

EVERYTHING SHIMMERED in the steamy air. The flies attacked us in droves as we ran up the bank to the graves. Miss G appeared again and told us to line up. It was getting late. It was time to go back.

She asked for Fiamma. When no one answered, she called her loudly, again and again, in her deep, mellow, man's voice. Then she sent us all off to search along the bank of the river, where she had last seen her. Fiamma was not on the edge of the bank in the high, wet grass, under the trees, in the picnic area, or on the dark, shiny rocks.

We called her name and received in reply the buzz of the flies and the scream of the cicadas, the cry of the sparrow hawk. We slapped at our legs, cheeks, and arms. We wiped the sweat from our brows. Miss G removed and wiped her steel-rimmed sunglasses with trembling hands and told us to search farther down the riverbed. The cuffs of her khaki jumpsuit were stained green, and there was red mud on her boots and her hands. She was smoking one cigarette after the other and stamping out the butts. She was striding up and down along the edge of the river. She was scratching again. She looked wild; her face and dark hair were streaked with red earth.

We ran down into the river, the damp sand seeping between our toes. The brown water looked so still we felt we could walk on it. We waded in up to our waists, looking behind rocks and rotted tree trunks and ferns, calling for her. Finally, exhausted, our clothes wet and our faces smudged and burned and bitten, we straggled back to Miss G.

The sun was sinking as she blew her whistle and told us to line up. She marched the twelve of us in silence, double-file, back across the muddy veld.

The search

IT STARTED RAINING hard again after we got back. Following months of drought, the constant rain turned the veld to mud, washed away the thin topsoil, eroded the land, and swelled the rivers. It rained on and off for days, making the search for Fiamma increasingly difficult.

Search parties were sent out with bloodhounds, as Miss Nieven had informed us they would be; they combed the long, wet grass all along the banks. The next day the river was dragged. The police searched the area for miles around. An advertisement was placed in the local papers with a photo of Fiamma in her school uniform, her swimming team badge, and her panama hat with the brim turned down so that the shadow fell on her face. It mentioned something we had never noticed, a strawberry-shaped birthmark on her shoulder. Someone reported hearing screams coming from the graves.

The detective questioned us again, this time as a group. We repeated what Di had already told him, that the last we saw of Fiamma was her lying very calmly in the shade of the frangipanis.

John Mazaboko, too, was questioned by the detective, because he knew the area where Fiamma had last been seen. It was he who tended the graves. We presumed he had not noticed anything unusual, or at any rate had not seen fit to say anything about it to the detective. But whether he had reported anything further to Miss Nieven, which she had felt it wiser not to pass on, we were never to find out.

No one mentioned Miss G.

Miss G's departure

MISS G DROVE OFF in her old, square, maroon Buick as we watched from the same dormitory window from which we had watched Fiamma arrive. Only Di went to say good-bye. We saw them sitting on the red polished steps between the sandstone lions for a moment, before Miss G rose, squared her shoulders bravely, soldierlike, and strode off to her car in her lacquered boots.

Afterward we asked Di what Miss G had said to her. Did she mention where she was while we played the game of truth? Had she heard what Fiamma had said?

Di told us that Miss G had said that she could understand very well why she had been fired. "They needed a scapegoat, and, of course, it had to be me. With their inhibited imaginations, they could not simply accept that she had disappeared. Why, she might have gone off anywhere. Anywhere there is a scandal, someone's head must roll."

Di went on to say that she had objected strenuously. "The injustice of it! After all those years of hard work. This school has never had such a successful swimming team. All those trophies we won for them! And all because of your coaching. You would have left anyway, I know, after what happened. You always sacrificed yourself for us."

Our parents' reaction

MISS NIEVEN EXPERIENCED a brief period of difficulties after Fiamma's disappearance. When the name of the school was linked to the disappearance in several articles that appeared in the local papers, there were long telephone calls; telegrams arrived in stacks. There were descriptions of Fiamma's prominent family, the area where she disappeared, the isolation and lack of supervision in our school.

The *Johannesburg Star* wrote indignantly: "What was a band of innocent young girls doing, marching for miles across bare veld in the burning heat? Why were they left to their own devices by the banks of a bilharzia-infested river? Where were the teachers? And all of this during the polio scare, which has already wrecked so many of our precious children's lives."

Initially, many of the girls' parents threatened to take them out of the school. Meg's father arrived and wanted to take all five girls home. A teacher himself, he had driven up all the way from Barberton. We watched him jump out of his battered old car in the driving rain, slamming the door, holding his worn tweed jacket with the patches on the elbows to cover his and his wife's heads, though covering more of his than hers, so that her hair clung to her damp forehead. He charged ahead, driven by righteous indignation — how could the school have been so negligent? — ascending the stairs two at a time, dragging his frumpy and faded wife between the sandstone lions, dispatching her to pack up the girls' belongings in their cardboard suitcases and to wrap up their books in brown paper parcels.

He closeted himself with Miss Nieven in her study. She had just placed a frantic call to the hospital where Fiamma's father was confined with his recurrent fevers, trying to communicate to him what she knew, and to gather his responses.

She persuaded Meg's father to leave the girls by hinting that Meg would most likely become head girl, and she did; most of the other parents eventually followed suit. It was said that if a father of five had confidence in our school, the other parents could too. None of our parents came to take us home.

Our reactions to Fiamma's disappearance

DI SAID she could not feel anything, anymore; nothing made her sad or happy. Meg acquired that blank look in her sloe eyes. She told everyone she was going to marry a rich husband, and of course, she did. Sheila stopped telling stories of doom and destruction at night in the dormitory. It was only many years later that she dared to take up her pen again, and then only to write thrillers. Mary gave all her horse books to the twins and said she was never going to ride again. Lizzie said she would become a librarian and found work in a bookstore. Fuzzie sat and stared in silence. But it was Ann, our Logical Lindt, who was the one who could not get over the loss. Sobs shook her thin body through day and night. Mrs. Looney sent her to the san, but the respite did not help. After some weeks Miss Nieven wired her parents, and she was sent alone on the endless train ride back to Salisbury. She went back to the mother who had drooping bosoms and hair on her upper lip and a maths degree from Oxford.

Ann was told not to take her books along, because she had overreached herself. Her weeping was put down to excessive reading and ambition. She was given a piece of cross-stitch and told to do it on the train and to lie down in her room on her arrival with the curtains drawn. She told us she stuffed the cross-stitch down the back of her train seat.

None of us wanted to stay on the team, now that Miss G was gone. We dropped out, one by one. We became studious, diligent. We took to listening in class and copying down exactly what the teachers said. We repeated their words verbatim in our examination papers. We toned down our natural rebelliousness. We wore pale powder to cover our blemishes. We walked in silence down the long corridors, our heads lowered slightly, our gaze on the ground, our books clutched to our chests. Even Di spoke softly, and blushed, and began stooping to hide her height. We spent our time bent over our books, trying to absorb all the facts we had avoided until then, too busy swimming for Miss G and God.

We spent our free time preparing for the school dance. Some of our parents ordered our dresses from overseas. Di's white, strapless dress, which showed off her smooth, broad shoulders, came from Harrods, Sheila's, from Liberty's. Meg made her own dress out of pink taffeta and sewed seed pearls around the high neck, and she looked lovelier than anyone else.

We decorated the hall with an Oriental theme: we put fans on the walls and Chinese lanterns around the lights. We invited boys this time, and we rehearsed the presentation of our choices to Miss Nieven over and over. Sheila kept muttering, "Miss Nieven, this is Mark Bell. Miss Nieven this is Mark Bell," as she walked up and down the pergola, but when the time came, she said, "Mark Bell, this is Miss Nieven."

Miss Nieven wore a long Black Watch tartan skirt and a black velvet top. To our surprise and amusement, she joined in when we did the hokeypokey. She put her left foot in, took her left foot out, then shook it all about, lifting her scrawny arms and turning herself. We all joined in.

Our bodies had grown soft, curvaceous, by then. We lolloped around in the water and tittered for effect. No one swam the crawl, that powerful oceangoing stroke; we swam sidestroke or breaststroke, or we did not swim at all. We all feared muscles in our arms and legs. We decided that what Miss G had had to teach us was not very useful for the business of living, after all. We were too old for cracks now. We were worried about our future. Some of us wanted to go on to the universities, where we hoped to meet a mate.

We no longer ran across the veld out-of-bounds to the river and the graves. We avoided the graves. We never climbed up on the grave and played dead again; we never played the game of truth; we kept our secrets to ourselves. We had no secrets; we no longer dreamed, or if we dreamed, it was of boys, real boys with crew cuts and thick white socks and thick-soled boots.

PART SIX

REMEMBRANCE

✦✦✦

Sunday morning

IT IS ALREADY HOT, and the palms beyond the window rustle. We sit in the dining room and sip our tea from tin mugs that scald our lips. There is the familiar odor of oranges and dust.

Ann's gray hair is still wet from her shower and falls over her high, shiny forehead. She cracks open an egg, and her small eyes squint in the bright light. Fuzzie has forgotten to brush her hair. She dusts bread crumbs from her chest. Di stares in gloomy silence, writing with a thick silver pen. She coughs her smoker's cough. Meg and Mary, still late sleepers, have not yet come down from the dormitory.

Miss Nieven wanders in for a moment, wearing the same mauve dress with the amber beads, as though she has not slept all night. She hovers, a dark figure, with the sun at her back. She looks so frail we feel death could come at any moment and whisk her away from the thin anchorage of her cane. She whistles as she wishes us a good day. We start to rise from our seats, scraping back our chairs as we did so many years ago, but she gestures to us to sit down. We expect her to say grace as she always did: "For what we are about to receive, may the Lord make us truly thankful," but instead, she suggests we take a picnic to the riverbank. She says, "You will find the place quite unchanged," and she looks at us blindly, until Di rises and goes over to her and gives her our check. She clutches the folded paper in her knotted hands. She puts on thick glasses and opens it and holds it up close to read the sum and then slips it into her pocket. She leans toward Di and whispers something in her ear and kisses her cheek. She smiles at us, nods, and then wanders out the door into the bright light, tapping with her cane on the stone floor.

Fuzzie says she dreamed her old dream of the child drowning, but this time she knew it was Fiamma she was trying to rescue from the water. She was trying to hold on to her, but she was slipping from her arms. Her body was naked and slippery as though she were covered with grease, and she was falling down into the darkness at the bottom of the sea.

Di tells us how she met up with Miss G years later, when Di was out here to visit. She found Miss G sitting in a faded raincoat on the steps of a department store. Miss G rose and accosted her and insisted she have tea. They took the double-decker bus to her small but spotless studio in Hillbrow. Di had had no desire to have tea with her, but she had insisted. She told Di she had not been able to find work teaching after they fired her. She said she had been obliged to take a housekeeper's job. She kept feeding Di one slice of cake after another and bringing out more sandwiches and little packets of sugar she must have stolen from some tearoom.

She brought up Fiamma. She said that Fiamma, to her surprise, had thrown herself at her wildly. "The truth is, she seduced me. At fourteen she was no virgin. She knew how to go about it, I assure you. She was such an exasperating brat, after all, and yet . . ."

At the graves

THE MIXTURE of flies, mosquitoes, and heat is the same as it was years ago, as it is, everywhere, in places of this sort. We can hear the buzzing of the fat flies from the latrines — the kind with glossy, green wings — and the hum of the mosquitoes. "Enough to drive you mad," Ann says, as we all walk up from the riverbank toward the graves.

We are here together again, going through the long, wet grass and the low scrub, up the bank to the graves of Sir George Harrow and his dog, Jock. The gray-branched frangipanis still spread their pale blossoms. Nothing seems changed except the dog's gravestone, which has been spray-painted yellow.

First we talk, then we fall silent. It is the dead quiet we noticed when Fiamma first walked into the dormitory and stood there, blinking her dark eyelashes, and it all began.

We are crowded together around the cracked marble tombstone with its worn inscription. We can hear the soft gurgle of the slowly flowing water and the call of the dove. There is the dreamlike intensity of things.

Di stands at one end of Sir George's tomb and says, "Meg, perhaps you should say a proper prayer." Meg kneels down and recites the Twenty-third Psalm.

We all remember how Meg spread Fiamma's loose hair around her shoulders and crossed her hands on her still chest. We covered her slender body with the white irises that still grow here, and the honeysuckle that climbs around the tomb. We had never seen Fiamma look as lovely: her delicate features, her flaxen ringlets, her oval face — as exquisite a countenance as we had ever beheld, with her chin tilted slightly upward, as though there were something she still wanted to offer us.

Together we manage now to move the slab of heavy marble that covers the airtight tomb. We make an opening wide enough to slip through, as she did years ago. Dust rises in the air and drops onto the gray branches and leaves of the frangipani. We look down into the darkness, and see Sir George's bones, which have been lying there for so long, so peacefully. They are as white and dry as shells, and beside them lies another set, along with the scraps of brown tunic and the shriveled brown lace-up shoes.

We remember

WHILE FIAMMA was talking about Miss G during the game of truth, Di says she passed out. For a momemt Di saw black as Fiamma spoke about Miss G. When Fiamma said Miss G did not tell the truth, Di lost consciousness for a moment. When she came back to herself, she told Fiamma that if she could be Miss G's Madeline, she could be ours, too. "You have to be our Madeline now," Di said firmly and put her hand over Fiamma's mouth.

Fiamma started up and struggled with Di. They wrestled, holding on to each other, pulling and scratching and biting, but Fiamma was no match for Di. Di had her by the arm; she was twisting it. All Fiamma could do was escape from her grip. She broke loose and smacked Di hard across the face, panting. For a moment Di, stunned, stood motionless.

No one moved.

Fiamma ran from us. She bolted through the circle and ran

out of the picnic hut up the bank toward the graves. She ran as fast as she could in her brown tunic, her little camphor bag bouncing on her back, her heavy lace-up shoes sinking and slipping in the red mud, the long grass, wetting her legs but racing on in the steamy air.

Fiamma, who was so fast in the water, was not fast on land.

"After her," Di yelled. We shouted and rushed forward as a group, running through long grass and scrub, excited by the chase. "Madeline, Madeline, you are going to be our Madeline," we shouted wildly.

The shouting made us feel brave and reckless. Our faces were shouting masks. In the hot, steamy sunlight we were running and slipping and jumping over everything in sight: deep dongas, rocks. Our sweating bodies were close, but we were running separately, in our distinctive ways. Meg ran gracefully, her well-turned ankles and her wasp waist revolving swiftly; Di ran aggressively, long-legged, knobby-kneed, arms swinging; the twins, side-by-side, indistinguishable, snub-nosed, white-haired, their sinewy calves shining; Ann, spindly and thin, coming behind; Sheila, like an ostrich, as if on stilts; and finally Fuzzie, her peg legs visible in the glare. We were a pack, giving off high-pitched screams.

The sound of our voices came back to us, bouncing off the wattle trees. We were hot, feverish, nauseated. Our minds were blank. Our nerves were jangled from lack of sleep, the long walk, the singing, Fiamma's words. For a moment, we lost her under the trees. It was cooler and darker there. We all stopped and looked about, our eyes glinting. "Where did she go?" Di cried and wiped her forehead and blinked. We could see the red imprint of Fiamma's fingers on Di's cheek. The faint smell of Miss G's smoke hung in the air like a pall.

Then we heard a shallow cough.

Fiamma had flung herself down under a bush to steady her breathing. She was halfway up the bank.

"Leave me alone," Fiamma cried, as she staggered out into the bright light and up the bank toward the graves and the open air. We hesitated. Perhaps we would have given up. But then she tripped and fell over something.

We were onto her.

Meg, who was the fastest runner, caught up with her at the graves and gave her a playful tap on her behind. "Lie down and be our Madeline," she said, giggling, accustomed to watching her father beat her younger sisters.

Fiamma panted, clutching her throat, "Leave me alone. I can't breathe. Ann, make them go away," she begged and clambered up onto Sir George's tomb to escape. We were sure she was only pretending not to be able to breathe, just playing at being the victim, the martyr, once again.

Ann, who had followed along with the rest of us, still clutching her blue book in her hands, shook her head and said, "Too late, Princess Fiamma."

"Get her! Get her!" Sheila said, pulling a piece of long, wet grass from the ground and pretending to whip Fiamma's white legs. Fiamma jumped up and down on the gray marble as though she were trampling on grapes, kicking out at us as we slapped at her. She did not seem to understand that we were only playing.

"Smack her! Smack her!" Pamela shouted, grabbing a stick from the ground and waving it in the air. "Down, down, down on your bed, Madeline!" she commanded.

We were all gathered around now in the shade of the frangipani tree. Sweat blinded us. Our heads throbbed, and our mouths were dry. The mosquitoes swarmed in droves, biting our arms and calves. We smacked at them. We echoed Pamela, "Madeline, Madeline, you have to be our Madeline."

Fiamma's jiggling white legs made us giggle. She looked like a puppet on a string, her arms and legs jerking. Our eyes glinted with merriment. There was Princess Fiamma, her face streaked with mud and sweat, jumping up and down on the gray marble slab that covered the illustrious bones of Sir George. She had lost her velvet hair ribbon in the chase, and her pale hair tumbled crazily across her forehead and into her eyes. Her chest rose and fell. She was panting and wheezing.

Sheila was putting it all down in her head.

Fiamma's face was puce, and a thin trickle of blood seeped down her calf where someone had scratched her with a stick. The blood frightened her, and she whispered hoarsely, "Stop it, please. You are behaving like a bunch of barbarians." She was slowing down, as though treading water. She was jumping back and forth, from one side to the other of the tomb, driven by our hands, our sticks, and pieces of wet grass. She was breathing loudly.

Di was growing impatient. "Keep still! Do what you did for Miss G," she shouted and threw her stick hard at Fiamma. It caught her in the right eye. Fiamma lifted her hand to it and plumped down blindly on the marble. She lunged out at us and scratched and bit and pulled at hair; she kicked at us angrily, catching Di in the bosom.

"You idjut, you got my boosie!" she shouted, suddenly furious. "Get her! Get her!" she urged, and the twins jumped up onto the tomb. One on each side, they held Fiamma down.

"Go for the bum! Go for the bum!" Pamela shouted. Then we all took up the chant: "Go for the bum!"

When Fiamma tried to get up, the twins pushed her down hard, one on either side. They flipped her over onto her stomach and pulled up her tunic and smacked her behind with a stick. We all smacked her behind with sticks. Meg smacked harder and harder, yelling loudly, her dark hair falling into her eyes.

Fiamma was scratching and biting desperately, more and more frightened, and the more she fought, the tighter the twins were obliged to hold her down. If she had let us play with her, perhaps, nothing much would have happened. She tried to cry out, but only her ragged breathing escaped. Anyway, the only ones who could have heard her were the swimmers and God and, perhaps, Miss G.

"Give me a snot rag. Shut her up," Di shouted, while we all watched, fascinated. Di grabbed Ann's dirty handkerchief and shoved it into Fiamma's mouth. Her face was purple now, her eyes bloodshot. She was trying to say something or reach her inhaler with her waving hands, but Ann grabbed them and tied them with her tunic belt. Mary tied her feet together. Then all we could hear was Fiamma's ragged heaving and panting.

"Hey, quit hurting her, she can't breathe properly," Fuzzie said softly, but no one heeded. We did not let her through the circle we had formed around the tomb. We pushed Fiamma's gag further into her mouth, and someone pulled down her knickers, exposing her bare behind. She lay sprawled before us, a white doll, helpless, our plaything.

"I'm Porphyro, and she's my Madeline," Meg cried.

"Do her, do her," everyone chanted.

"Up the bum, up the bum," Di called out.

No one was paying attention to Fiamma's face.

In the blinding white light she lay on the marble tomb, our victim, bound hands and feet, as on an altar, with the priestess, Ann, brandishing her book, watching what was happening, the slaves gathered around the victim, leaning over her, the rest of us, inserting whatever came to hand — it was mainly sticks, though Lizzie, who was always more elegant than the rest, had found the stem of a wild rose — into Fiamma's behind. One by one we thrust something hard and sharp into her tight, child's orifices, while she gagged and tried to scream.

Swimming

WE STARE into one another's eyes from both sides of the grave, as though gathered around a table for an evening meal. Our faces are brought nearer by the light of the southern sunset. Our makeup has washed away. We wear no jewelry, no fancy clothes, no camouflage. We see the lines, the sag and fall, the indistinct, watery gazes. We see ourselves in one another's sad eyes, relieved that this reunion has ended. No one speaks.

A change goes through us: Meg slings an arm around Di's shoulder; Fuzzie hands Ann a handkerchief; Bobby Joe removes a burr from Bobby Jean's sleeve. For a moment we huddle together, as though the presence of one another can shut out the outside world, the watery wastes, the fast-encroaching dark.

We stand together and watch the sunset char the sky, as if for the first time. We look across the marble grave as the red light kindles the river's memory, sparks down the hills, flames the frangipanis, ignites the vast sky. Lit up, our small world widens.

Fuzzie suggests we swim the river. We mention bilharzia and the possibility of quicksand. She does not listen but runs through the lion-colored grass down the bank to the water. Her modesty vanishes in the blinding glare. Piece by garish piece, she strips. We notice she still wears her vest, as her mother told her to do, so many years ago. Fuzzie's milky, freckled flesh is still firm and fresh. Without her clothes she looks almost like the girl we remember from long before, the tender, plump body, tight in its pink skin, and the tight auburn curls. We watch her wade into the brown water and pat the surface with her palms. "It's warm. Come on in," she says and floats on her back, staring up at the blazing sky. Then she swims out to the middle of the river and dives down and comes up somewhere else. She keeps plunging.

The twins are the next to discard their identical long gray skirts and worn tennis shoes. Then everyone undresses. Ann removes her glasses, unbuttons her shirt, and says, "Oh, hell, why not?" You can still see her ribs, and her skin looks greenish in the glare. Even Di pulls off her dark dress and lace corsets, and rolls down the dark stockings she still wears. She lumbers into the water. Meg's bare body dazzles, her breasts still firm, her nipples pink, her stomach smooth. We splash one another and shout like the wild girls we once were.

We imagine Miss G striding up and down the bank, her yellow whistle between her lips, watching us swim, exhorting us to slice through the water, to knock them flat.

Meg swims sidestroke swiftly, going through the clinging reeds and the glistening rocks. She bobs up and down. Di does a fast crawl, avoiding rocks and rotted tree trunks and ferns. Sheila turns on her back and strikes out, stretching her arms straight, brushing her ears with her arms, kicking with the regular rhythm that Miss G taught her.

We all swim down the river. There is a distant call as of a dreamer's voice, clear and shrill. We go onward in silence, expectant.

Then, look, there she is, out there, kicking up a rainbow spray. We feel her presence drawing us on, as we swim fast, striking out bravely through the dark water.

We see Fiamma, our dead sister, our wild girlhood, our lost dreams. We watch her, so slow and languorous on land, cutting through the water, leading the way with easy, strong strokes. Then we clamber, naked, up the bank, and the sun dips behind the wattles.

We do not walk back the way we came. We take another path and go slowly across the flat veld beneath the darkling sky.